An Event-Based Science Module

VOLCANO!

Student Edition

Russell G. Wright

Innovative Learning Publications®

Addison-Wesley Publishing Company

Menlo Park, California • Reading, Massachusetts • New York
Don Mills, Ontario • Wokingham, England • Amsterdam • Bonn
Paris • Milan • Madrid • Sydney • Singapore • Tokyo
Seoul • Taipei • Mexico City • San Juan

The developers of Event-Based Science have been encouraged and supported at every step in the creative process by the superintendent and board of education of Montgomery County Public Schools, Rockville, Maryland (MCPS). The superintendent and board are committed to the systemic improvement of science instruction, grades preK–12. EBS is one of many projects undertaken to ensure the scientific literacy of all students.

The developers of *Volcano!* pay special tribute to the editors, publisher, and reporters of *USA Today* and the Cable News Network. Without their cooperation and support, the creation of this module would not have been possible.

Pages 2, 7, 9, 18, 22, 36, 37, 45, 48, 55, 56, *USA Today*; 7, 18, 36, 48, 55, AP/Wide World Photos; 3, 10, 25, 26, 29, 32, 39, 40, 54, USGS; 51, 52, 53, NASA; 4, Arthur L. Center, Outdoor Photographers League; 6, Washington Department of Natural Resources; 56, Irene Natividad, Philippine American Foundation
Managing Editor: Cathy Anderson
Project Editors: Katarina Stenstedt and Lois Fowkes
Production/Manufacturing: Leanne Collins
Design Manager: Jeff Kelly
Text and Cover Design: Frank Loose Design
Cover Photograph: John T. Barr, Gamma Liaison

This book is published by Innovative Learning Publications®, an imprint of the Alternative Publishing Group of Addison-Wesley Publishing Company.

This material is based upon work supported by the National Science Foundation under grant number MDR-9154094. Any opinions, findings, conclusions, or recommendations expressed in this publication are those of the Event-Based Science Project and do not necessarily reflect the views of the National Science Foundation.

All rights reserved. Pages 12, 15, 62, and 63 are designed to be used with appropriate duplicating equipment to reproduce copies for classroom use. Permission is hereby granted to classroom teachers to reproduce these masters. For all other purposes, request permission in writing from the Event-Based Science Project; Montgomery County Public Schools; 850 Hungerford Drive; Rockville, MD 20850.

Copyright © 1997 by the Event-Based Science Project.

Printed in the United States of America.
ISBN 0-201-49590-2

1 2 3 4 5 6 7 8 9-DR-00 99 98 97 96

Contents

Preface	v
The Story	
Part 1	1
Part 2	23
Part 3	35
Part 4	44
The Task	10
Science Activities	
Pop Goes the Mountain	5
Toying Around with Topography	14
Through Thick and Thin	27
Here Comes the Mud	30
The Fax and Nothing but the Fax	37
Do You Tire of Fire?	49
Discovery Files	
Volcanic Land Forms	3
Anatomy of a Volcano	6
Benefits from Volcanoes	17
Plate Tectonics and Volcanoes	19
Products of Eruptions: Gas, Lava, Ash, and Volcanic Bombs	24
Geysers and Smokers	28
Danger! Pyroclastic Flows	29
Volcano Hazards Fact Sheet	31
The Rock Cycle	38
Volcano Monitoring and Prediction	39
The Attraction of Mount Vesuvius	43
Volcanoes and Global Climate Change	51
Out-of-This-World Volcanoes	52
Hot Tips for Living with Volcanoes	54
Myths and Beliefs about Volcanoes	55

On the Job
Geologist	8
Television Producer	16
Geological Engineer	33
Volcanologist	41
Two Special-Effects Experts	46

Interdisciplinary Activities
Math: Volcanoes and Volume	57
Social Studies: Hot Spots	58
Technology Education: Air Cruisin'!	59
Writing: Volcano!	60

Performance Assessment
Writing to Persuade	61

Resources 64

Acknowledgments 66

Preface

The Event-Based Science Model

Volcano! is a student booklet about earth science that follows the Event-Based Science (EBS) instructional model. You will watch "live" television news coverage of the eruption of Mount Pinatubo in the Philippine Islands and read *USA Today* reports about the event. Your discussions about the volcano will show you and your teacher that you already know a lot about earth-science concepts in this event. Next, a real-world task puts you and your classmates in the roles of people who must use scientific knowledge and processes to solve a problem related to the threat of volcanic eruptions. You will probably need more information before you start the task. If you do, *Volcano!* provides hands-on activities and a variety of reading materials to give you some of the background you need. About halfway through the module, you will be ready to begin the task. Your teacher will assign you a role to play and turn you and your team loose to complete the task. You will spend the rest of the time in this module working on that task.

Scientific Literacy

Today, a literate citizen is expected to know more than how to read, write, and do simple arithmetic. Literacy also includes knowing how to analyze problems, ask critical questions, and explain events, as well as apply scientific knowledge and processes to new situations. Event-Based Science allows you to practice these skills by placing the study of science in a meaningful context.

Knowledge cannot be transferred to your mind from your teacher's mind or from the pages of a textbook. Nor can knowledge occur in isolation from the other things you know about and have experienced in the real world. The Event-Based Science model is based on the idea that the best way to know something is to be actively engaged in it.

Therefore, the Event-Based Science model simulates real-life events and experiences to make your learning more authentic and memorable. First, the event is brought to life through television news coverage. Viewing the news allows you to be there "as it happened," and that is as close as you can get to actually experiencing the event. Second, by simulating the kinds of teamwork and problem solving that occur every day in our workplaces and communities, you will experience the role that scientific knowledge and teamwork play in the lives of ordinary people. Thus *Volcano!* is built around simulations of real-life events and experiences that affected people's lives and environments dramatically.

In an Event-Based Science classroom, you become the workers, your product is a solution to a real problem, and your teacher is your coach, guide, and advisor. You will be assessed on how you use scientific processes and concepts to solve problems as well as on the quality of your work.

One of the primary goals of the EBS Project is to place the learning of science in a real-world context and to make scientific learning fun. You should not allow yourself to become frustrated. If you cannot find a specific piece of information, it's OK to be creative. For example, if you are responsible for the interview with the "survivor" of a historic eruption, you might base your response on the real people and things you know about. When you write your script, you also might use some of the descriptions found in Student Voices.

Student Resources

Volcano! is unlike a regular textbook. An Event-Based Science module tells a story about a real event; it has real newspaper articles about the event and inserts that explain the scientific concepts involved in the event. It also contains Science Activities for you to conduct in your science class and Interdisciplinary Activities that you may do in English, math, social studies, or technology education classes. In addition, an Event-Based Science module gives you and your classmates a real-world task to do. The task is always done by teams of students, with each team member performing a real-life role while completing an important part of the task. The task cannot be completed without you and everyone else on your team doing your parts. The team approach allows you to share your knowledge and strengths. It also helps you learn to work with a team in a real-world situation. Today, most professionals work in teams.

Interviews with people who actually serve in the roles you are playing are scattered throughout the Event-Based Science module. Middle school students who actually experienced the event tell their stories throughout the module, too.

Because this module is unlike a regular textbook, you have much more flexibility in using it.

- You may read The Story for enjoyment or to find clues that will help you tackle your part of the task.
- You may read selections from the Discovery File when you need help understanding something in the story or when you need help with the task.
- You may read all the On the Job features because you are curious about what professionals do, or you may read only the interview with the professional who works in the role you've chosen because it may give you ideas that will help you complete the task.
- You may read the In the News features because they catch your eye or as part of your search for information.
- You will probably read all the Student Voices features because they are interesting stories told by middle school students like yourself.

Volcano! is also unlike regular textbooks in that the collection of resources found in it is not meant to be complete. You must find additional information from other sources, too. Textbooks, encyclopedias, pamphlets, magazine and newspaper articles, videos, films, filmstrips, computer databases, and people in your community are all potential sources of useful information. It is vital to your preparation as a scientifically literate citizen of the twenty-first century that you get used to finding information on your own.

The shape of a new form of science education is beginning to emerge, and the Event-Based Science Project is leading the way. We hope you enjoy your experience with this module as much as we enjoyed developing it.

—Russell G. Wright, Ed.D.
Project Director and Principal Author

The Story—Part 1

Prelude to a Catastrophe

Mount Pinatubo is one of numerous volcanoes that lie around the edges of the Pacific Ocean. This string of volcanoes forms what is called the "Ring of Fire." Mount Pinatubo had been one of the quiet volcanoes in the ring for more than 600 years. But in early 1991, rumbles shook the area on central Luzon Island in the Philippines. Pinatubo, one of 22 officially active volcanoes in the Philippines, was stirring. On April 2, 1991, an explosion crackled through the air near Mount Pinatubo, destroying a square kilometer of forest near the Pinatubo summit.

Following this first explosion, a line of vents opened to spew columns of smoke and gas into the atmosphere. The smell of rotten eggs swept down from the upper slopes of Pinatubo. These were the early warning signals of the great eruption to come.

These events at Pinatubo did not go unnoticed. Officials at the Philippine Institute of Volcanology and Seismology rushed to the mountain. They set up a seismometer to monitor the shakes and groans of the volcano. American volcanologists were asked to assist by bringing more advanced equipment to better watch the volcano's deep inner rumblings. By the end of the month, Mount Pinatubo was dotted with a network of instruments to report hourly on its condition.

Throughout May, Philippine islanders felt hundreds of tremors. Seismic activity near the mighty mountain intensified. The volcano belched into the air an estimated 500 tons a day of sulfur dioxide (SO_2) gas, which was soon followed by as much as 5,000 tons each day. These events were sure indications that magma was rising from deep within Mount Pinatubo. Scientists spotted oozing molten

STUDENT VOICES

I didn't take the warnings seriously until we were actually in the car on the way to Subic Bay Naval Base.

During the eruption, it was black and the trees kept breaking. Every five minutes a tree would crack and fall from the weight of the ash. We were told to stay inside, because of the snakes and monkeys looking for food. But inside, the floor kept moving from the earthquakes, and that was scary. I don't want to live near another volcano ever again. One volcano is enough for me.

We have become a lot closer as a family. My little sister and I don't fight as much. I love my family more.

If I were making a television show about volcanoes, I would want to show how scary it really was. Two little girls died at the school where we stayed.

SHANNON SINNETTE
OMAHA, NE

rock during helicopter flights over the area, and they saw it streaming from a new dome on the mountain.

In early June, instruments recorded a large tremor. Scientists saw this quake as another warning from a mountain that last erupted in 1315. The seismic activity escalated even more. Nine days later, fumes discharged skyward more than 19 kilometers (12 miles) above Mount Pinatubo—yet another omen of bad things to come. ■

Discussion Questions

1. What are volcanoes and what causes them?
2. What kinds of things come out of a volcano?
3. Are all volcanoes the same?
4. Have there ever been volcanoes near your school? How do you know?
5. Will there ever be volcanoes near your school? Why or why not?

IN THE NEWS

Volcano threatens U.S. base

By Juan J. Walte
USA TODAY

The U.S. military today ordered the evacuation of Clark Air Base in the Philippines after a volcano — dormant for 611 years — erupted Sunday.

A total of 14,000 U.S. military personnel and dependents were ordered to leave — 2,000 troops were staying behind, for now, to guard the base.

Children clutched their dogs and babies clung to dolls as cars packed with household utensils, sleeping bags and luggage left for Subic Bay Naval Base, 50 miles to the south. Aircraft flew out Sunday.

The convoy stretched for nearly a mile as the first vehicles arrived at Subic today.

There was no sign how long the evacuees would stay but they were told to take three days worth of food, water and clothing, and important papers.

The volcano, Mount Pinatubo, is 8½ miles west of Clark. It hasn't erupted since 1380.

Philippine radio said the sky near the mountain was "like the night." Rock, ash and searing gas were being ejected.

Raymundo Punongbayan of the Philippine Institute of Volcanology and Seismology, today said "stronger eruptions are imminent."

Clark, a supply center for U.S. forces during the gulf war, and Subic Bay figure in stalemated talks between Washington and Manila over the U.S. military presence in the Philippines. At issue:

▶ How long should the United States keep forces there?
▶ How much should it pay?

Pinatubo is the second volcano along the Pacific Ocean's Ring of Fire to erupt in the past week. Residents near Mount Unzen in Japan are fearful of more avalanches after an eruption killed at least 37.

Seismologists said the eruptions were coincidental.

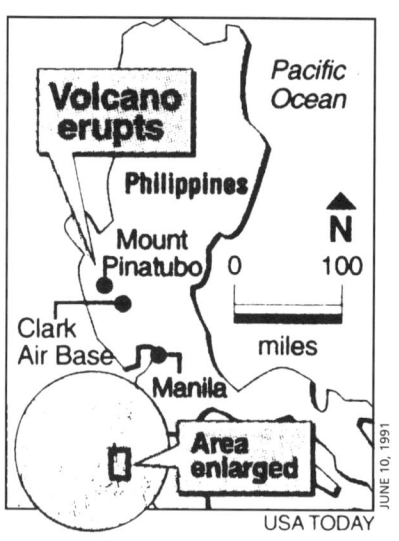

2 Volcano!

DISCOVERY FILE

Volcanic Land Forms

Volcanoes can take many forms—from to-wering peaks, to ex-pansive sheets, to small craters you can jump over. Shapes vary with the violence of eruption, the material tossed out, and the effects of erosion. There are four major types of volcanic land forms.

1. **Ash and cinder cones** develop when a powerful eruption ejects solid fragments from a crater. The solid particles fall back to the area around the vent. These concave cones are rarely more than 300 meters (1,000 feet) high. Craters of the Moon National Monument in Idaho contains many examples of ash and cinder cones.

2. **Lava cones** typically form from slowly rising lava. There are two main types:

   a. **Steep-sided volcanoes** such as Lassen Peak in California and Puy de Dôme in France were formed by sticky lava that quickly hardened. Squeezed out like toothpaste, this very thick lava creates spines as the lava solidifies in the "pipes" inside a volcano.

   b. **Shield volcanoes** are moderately sloping domes formed from runny lava that flowed some distance from its source vent before it hardened. One example of a shield volcano is Hawaii's Mauna Loa. Mauna Loa emerges from a seabed base that is about 250 kilometers (150 miles) across and rises gradually 9,750 meters (32,000 feet) to the immense crater at its summit.

3. **Composite volcanoes,** or stratovolcanoes, are cone-shaped and have concave sides. These cones are formed by alternating layered deposits of ash and lava. Most of the highest volcanoes on Earth are composite cones. Mount Fuji, Kilimanjaro, Mount Rainier, and Vesuvius are four well-known composite cones. Can you find these well-known volcanoes on a world map?

Mount St. Helens, two years after the eruption. By Lyn Topinka, USGS

If lava cools, hardens, and plugs the main pipe to the crater, pent-up gases may blast the top off a volcano, leaving a large hole. Or, if the magma chamber is emptied by a gradual flow, the summit may collapse. Either way, what's produced is a broad shallow crater called a *caldera*. Well-known calderas include Crater Lake in Oregon and Tanzania's Ngorongoro Crater. The largest caldera in the world is Japan's Aso, which has a 112-kilometer (71-mile) circumference.

4. **Basalt plateaus,** or lava plains, are born where fissures leak repeated flows of silica-poor lava. These lavas contain a large proportion of metallic elements and very little

The Story—Part 1

silica. They flow freely and erupt gently. They blanket large areas. Plateau basalts are fine-grained, igneous rocks with abundant, dark-colored minerals. India's Deccan Plateau is formed of a basalt lava flow totaling 2,100 meters (7,000 feet) thick and spanning an area of 650,000 square kilometers (250,000 square miles). Similar outflows form the U.S.'s Columbia River Plateau, South America's Parana Plateau, East Africa's Abyssinian Plateau, and Northern Ireland's Antrim Plateau.

Atolls

An atoll is usually a circle or broken circle of coral islands formed around a volcanic island in the open ocean. An atoll evolves from a fringing reef that becomes a barrier reef and then an atoll as the reef grows and the volcanic island subsides beneath sea level. Coral reefs are limestone rock created by the tube-shaped skeletons of billions of coral polyps—animals resembling tiny sea anemones. New organisms add their external skeletons to the skeletons of old, and reefs grow up and out. If sea level rises, a reef can grow higher and higher. If sea level falls, a reef can become exposed to wave erosion.

Scientific studies show that Eniwetok Atoll in the Pacific Ocean grew upward from a volcanic island now more than 1,400 meters (4,600 feet) below the surface. Most atolls are located in the Pacific and Indian Oceans. The Marshall Islands in the South Pacific include the world's largest atoll, Kwajalein, more than 274 kilometers (170 miles) long.

By Arthur L. Center, Outdoor Photographers League

Paricutín, located 180 miles west of Mexico City, first erupted February 20, 1943, out of a farmer's cornfield after a violent earthquake. In six days, it built a cinder cone more than 500 feet high. It destroyed two villages and damaged nine others. In 1952, all activity in the volcano ceased. It has formed a cone 1,345 feet high. It is said to be the first volcano to form in the Western Hemisphere since 1759.

SCIENCE ACTIVITY

Pop Goes the Mountain

Purpose

To build a model of a volcanic caldera and to observe and record changes and relationships.

Background

During your volcano research, you have made many contacts with volcanologists, geologists, cartographers, and other scientists. You have sent letters and received a great deal of information. Data sheets, books, rock information, graphs, and pictures are flooding your office. Each correspondence is full of helpful hints. The famous, though absent-minded, professor Dr. U. Candewit has also responded. Her letter is shown to the right, below.

Materials

For each group:
- Metric ruler
- Sand
- Gravel
- Several small balloons
- Tape
- Long pin
- Large box
- Colored paper
- Goggles for each group member

Optional for the class:
- Flour
- Pepper
- Spray bottles of water

Procedure

Dr. Candewit's letter is not very complete. She forgot the most important part, the instructions. You have a fairly complete list of materials, but it's up to you to develop a procedure to show caldera formation and carry out the experiment. Compare your procedures to those of other groups and refine your experiment. Keep careful measurements to determine whether any relationships exist between caldera formation and explosions. Don't forget to wear eye protection while viewing the "explosions" you create.

Conclusion

1. List the variables in your experiment. How does each relate to the others?
2. Use your model to explain the forces that can cause a volcanic explosion. How does this relate to the real thing?
3. Did the top of your "mountain" always explode? If not, what portions of the mountain exploded?
4. Choose a historic caldera formation. Write a brief description of it and use it in your production.

Dear Production Team,

You have asked me to suggest a good demonstration of caldera formation. As you know, calderas are sometimes formed by explosive eruptions. Explosions are usually due to the buildup of steam and other gases in the magma chamber under the volcano. To demonstrate one of these explosions on your show, you will need a metric ruler, sand, gravel, small balloons, tape, a long pin, large boxes, and colored paper. Once you get the hang of it, you can add materials such as flour, pepper, and other things to prove your point.

I hope I haven't left anything out of these instructions because I'm going on expedition to Indonesia and I won't be able to be contacted for a year.

Sincerely,

Dr. U. Candewit

The Story—Part 1

DISCOVERY FILE

Anatomy of a Volcano

When you think of a volcano, your mind might conjure up a heaving mountain of steam, lava, and rock. But volcanoes take on two main forms. **Fissure** or linear volcanoes give off lava from a crack in Earth's crust. **Central-vent** volcanoes produce lava, ash, or other products from a single hole. This ejected material develops into a shield-shaped or cone-shaped mound—the more familiar shape of a volcano.

Central-vent volcanoes can grow high very rapidly. For instance, in 1943, Paricutín volcano in western Mexico grew 154 meters (500 feet) in a week and reached 450 meters (1,500 feet) in just one year. Another central-vent volcano, the dormant Nevados Ojos del Salado in northern Chile, reaches 6,887 meters (22,595 feet) above sea level. It's the highest volcano in the world.

If you could split open an active central-vent volcano, you would see the magma chamber a few miles below the surface. The magma chamber is a reservoir of gas-rich molten rock under pressure. The pressurized magma pushes outward against the surrounding solid rock. The pressure is relieved when the magma blows through a weak point in the crust above. Magma then rises from the magma chamber through a central shaft. It sometimes shoots high into the air.

The ejecta from a volcano can be lava or rock fragments that range in size from fine-grained ash to huge blocks.

As the force of gases ruptures Earth's surface, a circular vent is formed. Ash and cinders are tossed out and then join with flows of lava to build the main volcano shield or cone. Explosions around the vent shape its top into an inverted cone or crater. Meanwhile, vents on the side of a volcano may spew out ash or lava and form additional cones. The randomness of these events makes each volcano different, just as each person's fingerprints are unique.

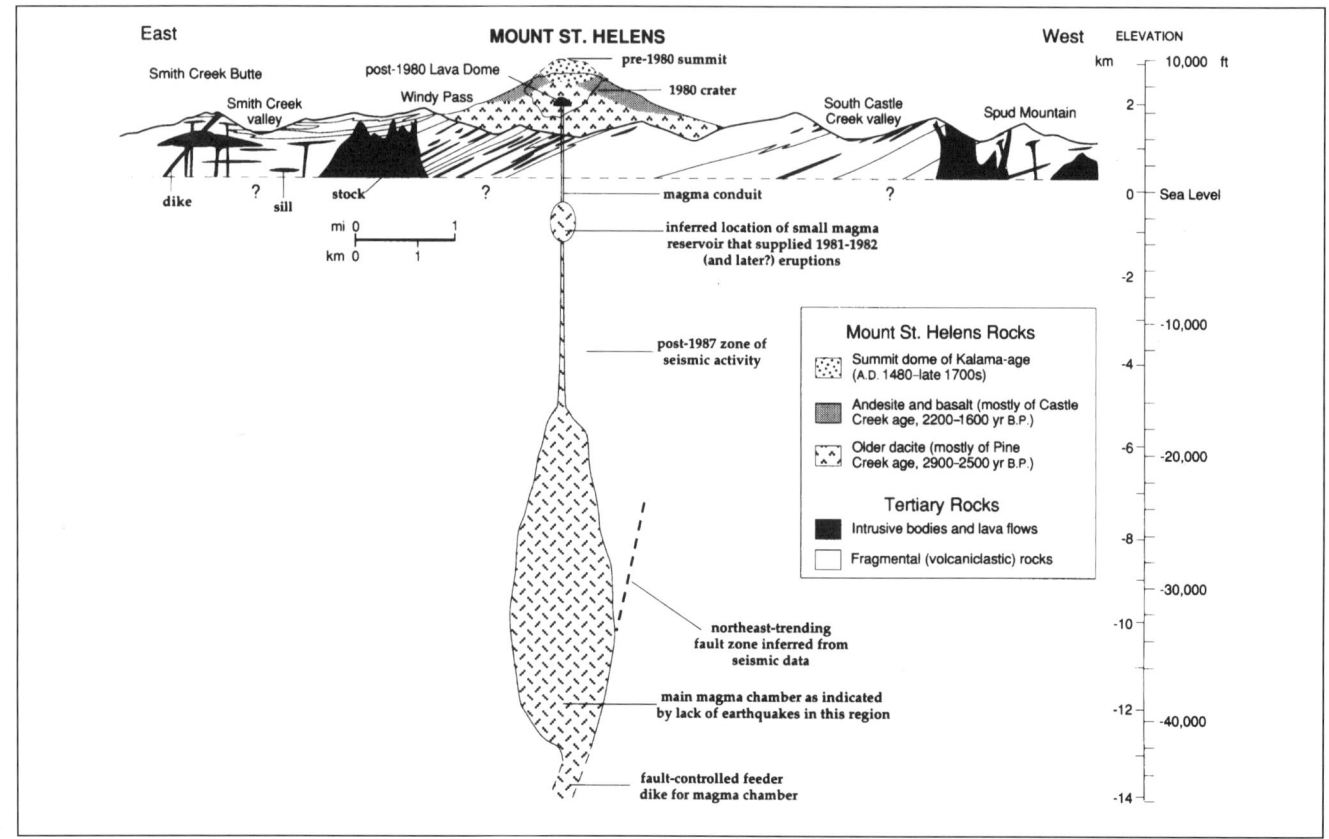

Washington Department of Natural Resources

Volcano!

IN THE NEWS

Filipinos running scared

Typhoon adds to eruption chaos

By Karen Emmons
Special for USA TODAY

MANILA — Hundreds of thousands of Filipinos fled the eruption of Mount Pinatubo Sunday, flooding roads in scenes reminiscent of World War II evacuations.

The volcano's eruptions showered a wide area with gray ash. The ash clouds blocked out the sun.

Terrified Filipinos, many clutching umbrellas in hopes of warding off falling ash and rocks, fled in a chaotic exodus.

Fortunato de Hora, director of the Philippine Office of Civil Defense, said it was impossible to determine how many people had fled their homes but that the number must be "in the hundreds of thousands."

A weekend typhoon added to the tumult, flooding rivers that washed away four bridges. The driving rain turned the spewing ash to a heavy gray muck that caused scores of rooftops to cave in.

Coarse ash fell on Subic Bay Naval Base — where about 20,000 Americans prepared to leave — mixing with thick, soupy mud, sometimes up to a foot deep. About 100 buildings collapsed at Subic, killing a Filipino maid and the child of a U.S. enlisted man.

The badly overcrowded Navy base now has no electricity. Water works only intermittently, officials said. Volcanic ash coated the ground.

Only a handful of U.S. military personnel have returned to Clark Air Base, now maintained by a skeleton crew of Americans.

Dozens of buildings and trees have collapsed, base officials said. The base — including runways, taxiways and roads — are caked with a 6-inch crust of ash.

"It's a wasteland," said Brig. Gen. Leopoldo Acot, the Philippine vice commander at the base. Break-ins and some looting were reported at Clark, which was left unguarded for a time by U.S. troops.

"You expect people will take advantage of the situation," Acot said on Sunday. "There were some break-ins. We don't know how many."

TRYING TO EVACUATE: Filipino family members sit by their stalled car Sunday watching thousands of others flee. Angeles, in the shadow of Mount Pinatubo, has a population of 188,000.

By Jeff Widener, AP

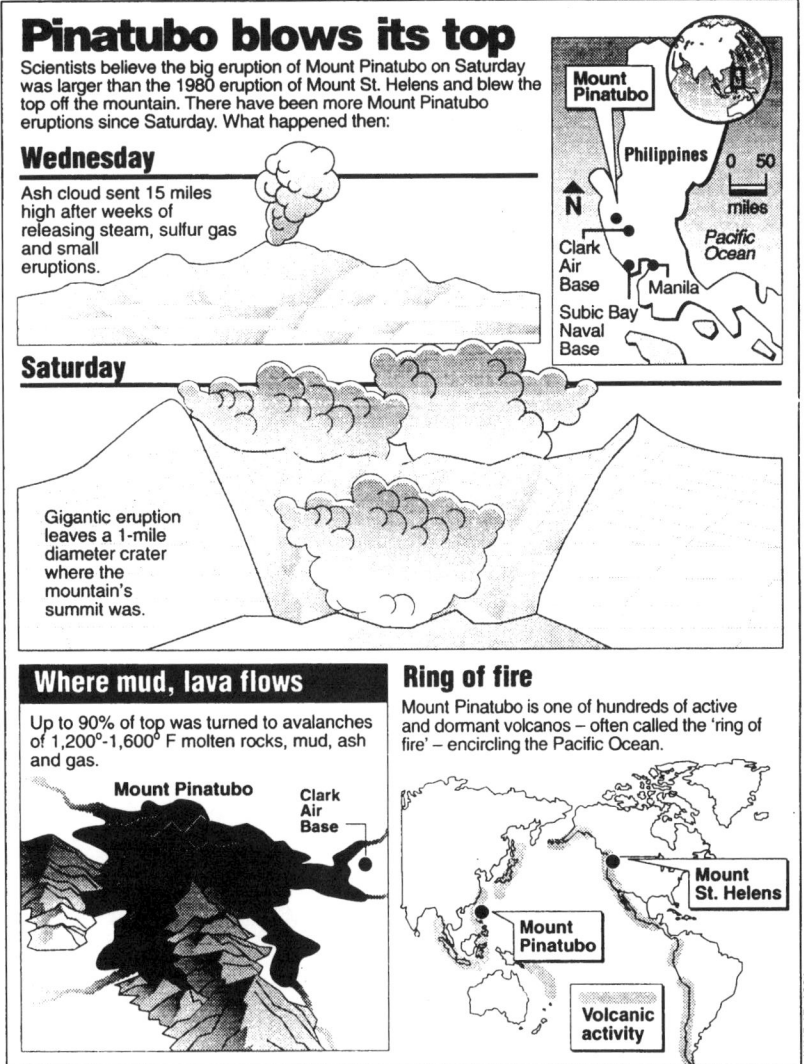

Pinatubo blows its top

Scientists believe the big eruption of Mount Pinatubo on Saturday was larger than the 1980 eruption of Mount St. Helens and blew the top off the mountain. There have been more Mount Pinatubo eruptions since Saturday. What happened then:

Wednesday
Ash cloud sent 15 miles high after weeks of releasing steam, sulfur gas and small eruptions.

Saturday
Gigantic eruption leaves a 1-mile diameter crater where the mountain's summit was.

Where mud, lava flows
Up to 90% of top was turned to avalanches of 1,200°-1,600° F molten rocks, mud, ash and gas.

Ring of fire
Mount Pinatubo is one of hundreds of active and dormant volcanos – often called the 'ring of fire' – encircling the Pacific Ocean.

Source: USA TODAY research; U.S. Geological Survey; World Book Encyclopedia   USA TODAY

ON THE JOB

Geologist

PAT PRINGLE
WASHINGTON DEPARTMENT OF NATURAL RESOURCES
SEATTLE, WA

I am a geologist for the state of Washington's Department of Natural Resources. I work in the environmental geology section of the Division of Geology.

When I was younger, I picked up rocks and wondered why they were there and where they came from. I grew up in an area of Ohio that was covered by glaciers during the last ice age. A quarry near my home had lots of different rocks that had been carried down from Canada by glaciers. I loved being outdoors and watching natural processes at work. These experiences helped shape my interest in geology.

My work today is quite varied. I respond to different kinds of geologic hazards: earthquakes, landslides, and volcanoes. Especially over the last several years, my work has become more involved with environmental education. Scientists in my field of research are trying to grow out of the habit of just talking to one another about what is going on in geology. More and more, we are sharing our work with policy makers, land-use planners, students, and the general public.

One of the exciting things about living in this part of the country is we have a "backyard volcano"—Mount St. Helens. Having this volcano nearby means a lot of tourists visit us.

Seeing Mount St. Helens erupt makes other eruptions more meaningful wherever they occur. Mount St. Helens also offers a good comparison with Mount Rainier. Rainier is a mile higher in elevation and topped by a tremendous volume of snow and ice.

From talking to various groups, it seems to me that people in general don't have a good understanding of the various volcanic processes and how they can be hazardous. Also, people don't seem to know that volcanoes can behave in different ways.

If I were making a television show about Mount Rainier, I would make a visual statement. I'd show Mount Rainier as a large glacier-clad volcano with an active geothermal system on its summit. In the show, I would include shots of the rivers that originate on the volcano. It would be important to show the layers of past lava flows and debris fragments deposited by older explosive eruptions. These former eruptions have built the volcano up to its present height.

In producing such a program, it would be very important to show how mudflows and pyroclastic flows can threaten valleys and towns around the volcano. The show could also include scenes from other volcanic eruptions to show the variety of activity and the different consequences that might result from different kinds of eruptions. Lastly, I would show the kinds of instruments used to monitor a volcano such as Mount Rainier and how these devices can be effective forecasting future eruptions.

As for those wanting to pursue a career in geology, taking earth science and geology classes are, of course, critical. Don't forget that communication and writing skills help you interpret and report your ideas and findings to others. Even artistic skills, such as sketching, add to the capabilities of someone doing science. It is very important to be able to communicate your insights to various groups, including journalists, to help educate everyone about geologic hazards.

Even if you don't pursue a career in geology, understanding geology and the earth's processes can add to your appreciation of what's going on around you.

For me, a typical day

depends on the type of geology I'm doing. If I am preparing a geologic map, I might be out in the field, perhaps spending a day, several days, or sometimes weeks to chart rock groupings and record other land forms in a notebook. Often, I am in the office looking at aerial photos with a stereoscope. This is an instrument that lets me view special aerial photographs in three dimensions. I can sit at my desk and actually feel as if I have a birds-eye view of the landscape. It helps me spot unusual things so when I go back out into the field, I can identify those features more quickly.

It's important to realize that geology has become more interesting in the last century. There has been a scientific revolution in the way we think about Earth in the last 30 or 40 years. We've discovered the vastness of geologic time and the role of plate tectonics in shaping Earth.

Geology is a youthful science: it continues to grow. That's why I like it so much. I'm always learning something new.

IN THE NEWS

Volcanic flow imperils base in Philippines

By Dianne Barth
USA TODAY

A Philippine volcano exploded today in a grey-greenish mushroom cloud of ash and molten lava, threatening to engulf nearby Clark Air Base.

There were no immediate reports of casualties.

The U.S. facility was evacuated earlier this week after threats of an eruption of Mount Pinatubo, 8½ miles to the west.

Pinatubo sprang to life Sunday, its first activity since 1380.

Today's explosion forced a skeleton guard detachment of 1,500 U.S. servicemen at Clark to flee for their lives.

▶ "You can feel the heat. Everywhere's covered in smoke," Reuter reporter Nerilyn Tenorio said by telephone.

▶ "This is very, very serious," said Reggie Okamura, chief of operations at the Hawaiian Volcano Observatory.

▶ "It's not safe within an 18-mile radius," said Raymundo Punongbayan, head of the Philippine Volcanology Institute.

But it was unclear whether this was the major eruption scientists had been predicting at Mount Pinatubo. Seismologists said pyroclastic materials — hot gas, rocks and other material — were racing down its desolate western slopes.

"Most probably there will be more eruptions," said seismologist Julio Sabit.

A plume of ash and steam was seen in Manila, 60 miles south. The eruption began at 8:51 a.m. (8:51 p.m. Tuesday EDT) with a huge explosion. Two smaller blasts followed.

Lt. Joy Sanchez, spokesman for the Philippine military's Clark Air Base Command, said there was a traffic jam in adjacent Angeles as thousands fled.

Church bells peeled to sound the alarm. Many people froze, then scampered for safety.

"The smoke is very thick... just like what we saw in Hiroshima," Gus Abelgas, of Filipino TV, reported from Botolan near the volcano's slopes.

JUNE 12, 1991

THE TASK

Volcano Warnings

The eruption of Mount Vesuvius in 79 A.D. brought a rather abrupt end to ancient Pompeii, killing many people and burying their bodies under millions of tons of ash. On the other side of the mountain, a city called Herculaneum was buried under mudflows and rains of hot mud.

Volcanoes don't spew forth lava only. Dust, "bombs," lava, and gases are all products of eruptions. Each of these can be deadly.

The eruption of Mount Pinatubo renewed peoples' concerns about living and working near volcanoes. The eruption hurled millions of tons of dust and gas into the earth's atmosphere. When the gas reached the stratosphere, it made particles that reflected incoming sunlight back into space and cooled the earth slightly for a few years. The particles also increased ozone loss from the stratosphere.

In the Philippines, as at Herculaneum, volcanic dust and ash mixed with rainwater and steam to form hot mud. Mudflows called *lahars* were common during and after the eruption of Pinatubo, and many people lost their lives as the hot ooze covered villages and homes. Clark Air Force Base closed during the eruption. It never reopened.

People living in the Pacific Northwest of the United States are also aware that volcanoes can be destructive. The threat of an active volcano in the region was driven home in the spring of 1980 when Mount St. Helens awoke from its 123-year sleep. The mountain began quietly rumbling in March and on Sunday, May 18, at 8:32 A.M. (PDT), a colossal bulge on the north side of the mountain suddenly collapsed, triggering an explosive eruption. It is now believed the collapse was triggered by an earthquake one mile below the surface.

By Lyn Topinka, USGS

A mudline left behind by the lahar of May 18. This is the scene along the Muddy River, southeast of Mount St. Helens

Nothing in the monitoring data suggested a catastrophe was about to occur. People saw Mount St. Helens not as a threat, but as a place to hike, camp, fish, and swim. After the violent eruption, one of the most destructive in the history of the United States, the image of tranquil Mount St. Helens changed. That eruption claimed 57 lives. Many were killed by asphyxiation when they inhaled hot volcanic ash.

Wildlife also suffered. Nearly 7,000 large animals such as deer, elk, and bears died in the blast. An estimated 12 million salmon fingerlings in fish hatcheries also died.

Downwind from the volcano, farmers lost income as volcanic ash damaged apples, wheat, and potatoes. More than 200 homes, 185 miles of highways, and 15 miles of railroad tracks were destroyed. As more ash fell, airports closed, canceling more than 1,000 commercial airline flights.

Washington State residents live in the shadows of potentially deadly mountains. They wonder whether other sleeping giants such as Mount Baker, Glacier Peak, Mount Adams, or Mount Rainier might someday come to life with the same disastrous results as Mount St. Helens.

Volcanologists focus their attention on volcanoes, looking for ways to monitor and better predict eruptions. Government officials in the state of Washington have similar concerns. Both groups are interested in preventing loss of life and property damage.

Producing a Television Show

Washington State officials are planning a new public-information campaign. The campaign will focus on risks related to Mount Rainier. Your media company has won the contract to produce a television show. The show will be broadcast as a 30-minute after-school television special. The target audience is middle school students.

Your contract is more open-ended than most. It allows you the freedom to be creative. It encourages your team to explore imaginative ways to capture the interest of middle school students. Scientific content of the program must be accurate, but because of the age of the target audience, the concepts and vocabulary must not be over their heads.

You will work as a member of a team that consists of

- a producer
- a special-effects expert
- a camera operator
- a volcanologist
- a geologist *or* a geological engineer

During the research phase of the task, all members of your team will help gather information. During the actual shooting, the production people will take over their roles related to videotaping, and the science experts (volcanologist and geologist) will be on screen or doing voice-overs to explain concepts.

When you first meet with your team, decide how you will divide the roles. The person chosen as producer will prepare a list of your team's members and their jobs and submit it to the executive producer (your teacher).

The program will be divided into six 4-minute segments. Your team will be responsible for one of the segments. Just before production time, your teacher will tell you which of the six segments your team will do. You will need to research all the segments in order to be prepared. In each segment, there must be mention of how the information in the segment relates to Mount Rainier.

You will need to keep a production log for each segment. The log should contain photocopies of all references (books, journals, government publications, interviews, and so on), lab data, sketches, and other materials used during your research.

A seventh segment will contain special effects of a volcanic eruption. This segment will be a joint effort of the special-effects experts from each team.

Production Segments

1. **Where are volcanoes located and how are they formed?**
   Topics:
   - Local and world-wide location of volcanoes
   - Relationship between earthquakes and volcanoes
   - Plate tectonics
   - Types of activity found along plate boundaries
   - Convection cells
   - Why is there a volcano where Mount Rainier is?

Volcanoes of Washington State

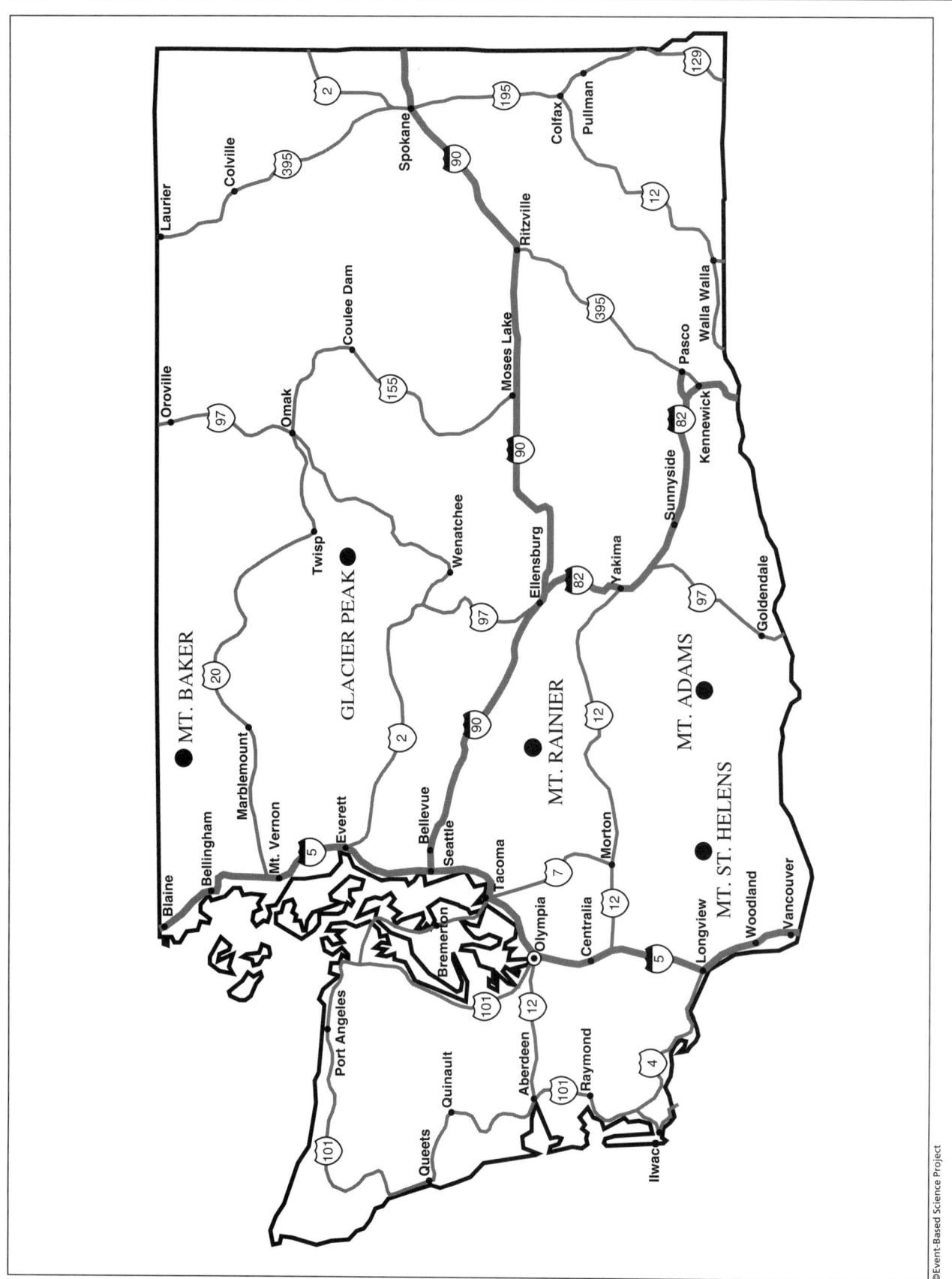

2. **How are volcanoes classified?**
   Topics:
   - What are their similarities and differences?
   - What are the different classifications of volcanic rocks?
   - What type of volcano is Mount Rainier?
   - What rock types are there?
   - Choose another volcano and classify it.
   - How is it similar to, and different from, Mount Rainier?

3. **What types of volcanic features are found above and below ground?**

4. **What are the effects, hazards, and benefits of volcanoes on people and the environment?**
   Topics:
   - Lava flows
   - Pyroclastic material
   - Volcanic gases
   - Landslides, mudflows, and debris flows
   - Tsunamis
   - Hot springs, geysers, and geothermal heat
   - Impact on the soil
   - Mineral formation related to volcanic activity
   - Industrial products made from volcanic materials

5. **How are volcanoes monitored?**
   Topics:
   Visual techniques

   Instruments and techniques used to understand volcanic processes and evaluate hazards posed by volcanoes

6. **Can eruptions be predicted?**
   Topics:
   - Earthquake activity
   - Ground movement
   - Gas release
   - Water level and temperature changes
   - Major risk to people living around Mount Rainier

STUDENT VOICES

We left Clark Air Force Base not knowing what was in store for us. We didn't even know if we'd ever go home or if we'd ever see our friends again.

I remember a woman who was allergic to sulfur; she couldn't go outside because of all the sulfur in the air. She had to be medevacked out.

I don't like uncertainty. I want to live somewhere where I have control to decide how long I will stay. I never want to live near a volcano again.

REBEKAH FITZGERALD
SPOKANE, WA

7. **Volcano eruption special effects**
   Show a model of an erupting volcano.

Optional segments:

8. **Volcanoes in history:** An account of one historically significant eruption anywhere in the world.

   Suggestions:
   Vesuvius, Krakatau, Nevado del Ruiz, Mount Katmai, Mount St. Helens, Mount Pelée, Santorini, and Mount Etna.

9. **An interview with a survivor of the historical eruption you select.** This part of the show will be fictional. Base the script for the interview on your research and the real words of students in Student Voices interviews.

Science Activity

Toying Around with Topography

Purpose
To build a model of Mount Rainier from a topographic map.

Background
A manufacturing company, Toys 4 U, has approached your project coordinator with a proposal for the production of a hands-on, do-it-yourself science kit. The kit will be a three-dimensional model of Mount Rainier. They plan to sell it in hobby shops and at the Mount Rainier visitor's center.

The company is interested in producing a variety of simple science kits students can use without needing special scientific equipment. If this project is successful, the company plans to develop models for other volcanoes, especially those considered to be historically significant.

Materials
For each pair:
- Topographic map of Mount Rainier (page 15)
- Scissors
- Poster board, cardboard, construction paper, and/or clay
- Pencil or pen
- Tracing paper
- Straws
- Masking tape
- Glue
- Toothpicks
- Metric ruler

Procedure
The project staff at Toys 4 U refer to this kit as a "paper-scissors" project that will require students to build "layers" to create the model. They want you to come up with directions that will enable students to go from the flat map to the three-dimensional model. Toys 4 U has done some preliminary thinking about the kinds of things that should be in the kit. They want you to include a map that will serve as a blueprint for the construction of the model. They will reproduce only the region of the main summit of Mount Rainier National Park, as the actual map is too large to be included in the kit.

General Guidelines
1. For packaging reasons, all items you produce must fit into a plastic bag that is 9 inches wide, 12 inches long, and ½ inch thick.
2. All your instructions must be clearly written and include diagrams that help the user complete the activity.
3. Instructions, maps, and other materials must not be folded.
4. The target age group is elementary grades 4 and 5.
5. Suggest materials that can be found around the house.
6. Compile a list of questions relating to the model and Mount Rainier.
7. Provide instructions aligning the layers so they fit together properly.
8. Create a section called Extension Activities to encourage students to construct additional topographic maps and models. These may be maps of the neighborhood or maps of imaginary places they create.

Conclusion
Organize all of the work you've prepared for Toys 4 U, and prepare a business letter to accompany your volcano kit. In your letter, comment on how appropriate this activity is for the age group your company is trying to reach and the educational value of your product. Deliver the following items to your teacher:
- Completed prototype model
- Completed instructions for the model
- Materials list
- List of questions related to the model
- Extension Activities

Topographic Map of Mount Rainier

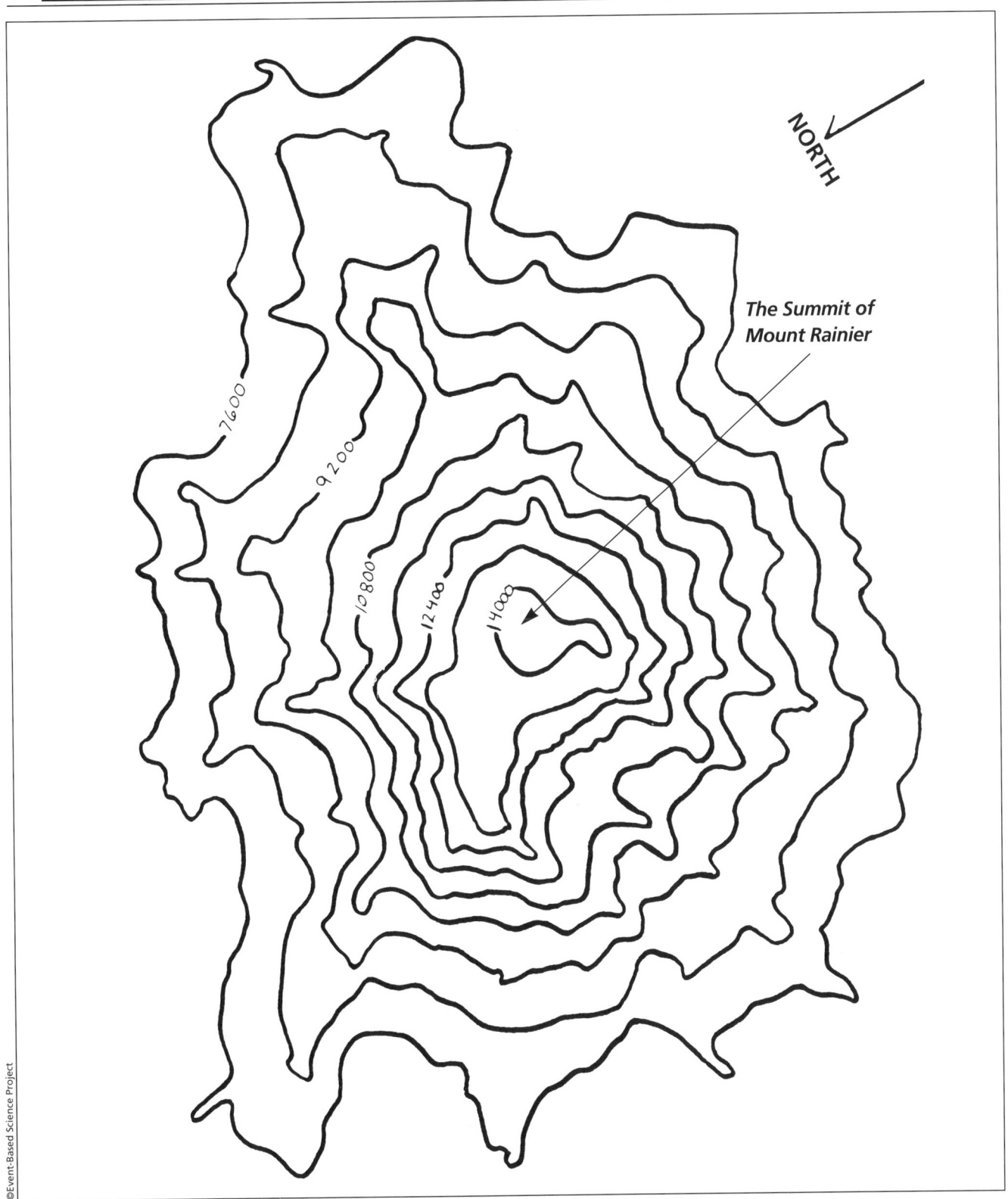

The Task—Part 1 15

On the Job

Television Producer

Rick Wilkinson
American Broadcasting Corporation
Washington, DC

I am a producer for ABC News and work on the weeknight show *Nightline* from our studios here in Washington, D.C.

My job takes me around the world. I've reported from such spots as Rwanda, Africa, Saudi Arabia, about 35 of the 50 states, and even Antarctica. Producing television from remote locations is exciting, challenging, and hard work.

When I was in junior high and high school, I certainly didn't think I would become a television producer, but my interests in pursuing this career began to be shaped there. I worked on my high school's closed-circuit television network. It was there I was introduced to electronic equipment such as video cameras and editing machines.

My interest in visual media led me to Syracuse University in New York State where I majored in television and radio. Those types of courses are really helpful if you want to work in the electronic media. Don't forget about working on your school newspaper. You've got to learn how to tell and write a story—something that has a beginning, middle, and end.

Taking up photography is also important. You learn what makes a good picture, and how best to use light, shadows, and composition. Remember, it's "tele" and "vision," so any course in visual arts as well as in writing is going to help you in a television career.

Understanding and knowing how to use technology is really important, too. Without technology, my story can't be told. My whole career is based on technology: from the cameras and editing equipment I used, to the jets that fly me to the story location, to the communication satellites that beam my story back to the station, to the televisions you watch. Knowing how to use computers is also important. All producers take laptop computers with them when they're in the field producing a story.

Before coming to ABC's *Nightline*, I worked on promotional videos that give you 5 to 30 seconds to get your point across. I guess it was from doing that work that I learned how to tell a story quickly.

Don't forget, this is about the story! Make sure technique doesn't get in the way of content. I have edited some very jumpy and choppy pieces. A lot of editing and music is not necessarily storytelling.

When I was in Zaire, I watched people fleeing Rwanda. People were dying everywhere. These people were starving and scared. We did several pieces from that location. In one of my stories, I left a shot on one scene for a good 15 seconds. That's much longer than you might normally do. Why did I do that? I did it so the viewer could look deeply into the eyes of this starving child instead of cutting away to show something else. Sometimes you have to stop and let a shot breathe. I can't explain when to do that. It becomes a matter of experience.

In my work to produce a piece for ABC, I use "A-roll" and

DISCOVERY FILE

Benefits from Volcanoes

"B-roll." These are old film terms that made their way into video. "A-roll" is when you're shooting an interview with the subject of the work, such as a volcanologist. Other footage of him or her in the field at a volcano, at the computer, or maybe explaining volcanoes to students is called the "B-roll."

If I were asked to do a piece on Mount Rainier, I would identify the most well-informed, articulate volcanologists and seismologists and ask them about the Mount Rainier situation. Some of these people might say an eruption is not likely to happen and there's no need to worry. Other scientists may be more concerned and worried about the consequences. I'd also try to find more colorful characters who live near the mountain, perhaps a poet or an artist. How worried are they?

Research time would be needed to study other volcanoes that may explode like Mount Rainier to find out any similarities. I would use "B-roll" of other volcanic eruptions, such as Mount Pinatubo or Mount St. Helens. You could use computer simulations to show what could happen if Mount Rainier erupted.

Finally, it would be important to talk to emergency-management people in the area. You would want to find out what evacuation plans would be used should Mount Rainier erupt. If there aren't any plans, ask them why no plans exist and when they will have them ready!

Volcanoes are one of the most destructive forces in nature. During the 1980s, more than 28,500 people died in volcanic eruptions. That's more people than were killed by volcanoes during the 78 years between 1902 (the eruption of Mount Pelée on the Caribbean island of Martinique) and 1980 (the eruption of Mount St. Helens).

They may be devastating, but volcanoes also produce many benefits. Active island volcanoes, such as Kilauea on the big island of Hawaii, are continually pouring out lava, increasing the size of the island, and creating more real estate. As volcanic ash becomes weathered and forms soil, the land becomes very fertile. On the slopes of Italy's Mount Vesuvius, the fertility is so great that farmers can sometimes produce three crops in a season instead of one.

Valuable ores and metals originate in magma and volcanic rock. Water seeps through the deep underground cracks that form in volcanic rocks. As it moves, it dissolves away minerals and metals. As these mineral-rich water solutions approach the surface—and temperature and pressure decrease—the solutions cool and crystallize. Veins of tin, copper, lead, zinc, iron, gold, and mercury have formed in this way.

Rock formed from lava is commonly used in building roads. Basalt and other lavas, as well as rocks derived from beds of volcanic ash that have hardened over time, were first used as building materials by the Romans around 100 B.C.

Obsidian, natural black glass, is not only fashioned into jewelry but was used by Native Americans for making knives and arrowheads. Pumice—the hardened froth of volcanic glass—is widely used for grinding and polishing stones, metals, and other materials. Sulfur deposits from volcanoes are used in making the chemicals that go into matches, gun powder, medicine, and vulcanizing rubber.

Underground steam is used as a source of energy in many areas of current or recent volcanic activity, often around the edges of tectonic plates such as the Pacific Ring of Fire. Geothermal energy plants produce electricity in Japan, New Zealand, Iceland, Italy, eastern Asia, Mexico, and the United States.

One of the world's largest geothermal facilities is The Geysers in California's Mayacamas Mountains, 145 kilometers (90 miles) north of San Francisco. In Reykjavik, Iceland, many homes are heated with water piped directly from volcanic hot springs.

Perhaps most important to Earth scientists such as yourselves, volcanoes are "windows" to the interior of our planet. By capturing and analyzing samples of volcanic gases, ash, and lava, we can begin to unravel Earth's inner secrets.

IN THE NEWS

Mt. Rainier eruption 'could kill thousands'

By Deeann Glamser
and Jack Williams
USA TODAY

SEATTLE — Mount Rainier is a seismically active volcano that could erupt anytime, a scientific report out Monday says.

"A major volcanic eruption ... could kill thousands of people and cripple the economy of the Pacific Northwest," says Richard Fiske, a geologist who led the National Research Council study.

But, Fiske says, the possibility of a Mount Rainier eruption in the very near future is remote. The last one was 150 years ago.

And in this city of sidewalk espresso carts and breathtaking views, people aren't overly worried about the volcano about 65 miles away.

"If I see plumes of smoke coming out of Rainier, I might start to worry," says salesman Jack McPherson.

Nevertheless, to protect the 2.5 million residents of the Seattle-Tacoma area, the report recommends:

▶ Added monitoring to detect unusual seismic activity.

▶ More attention to emergency preparedness.

▶ Changes in land-use policies in the areas most likely to be affected by an eruption.

Mount Rainier is part of the chain of Northwest volcanoes that includes Mount St. Helens, which erupted in 1980, killing 57.

Steve Malone, a University of Washington seismologist, says the mud and rock slide damage from a Rainier eruption could be "much greater than what happened at Mount St. Helens."

That's because Mount Rainier is closer to a large metropolitan area, and has 35 square miles of glaciers that could trigger huge mudslides.

To prepare, Fiske says, "scientists and officials are trying to carry out research before the crisis."

Some communities are taking the threat seriously.

Sumner, a town midway between Mount Rainier and Seattle, has a volcano evacuation plan for its schools, some built on a 1,000-year-old mudslide from Mount Rainier.

"We haven't practiced that evacuation, but in 10 to 15 minutes we could get the kids out," says emergency planner John Thomas.

The worst case would be an earthquake registering 7 or stronger on the Richter scale — "a disaster in its own right," Fiske says.

But, even in such a case, better monitoring might give enough warning for officials to empty reservoirs on rivers between the mountain and the metropolitan area, Fiske says. Mud could smash into emptied reservoirs without flooding dams.

Fiske says Seattle and Tacoma don't have to worry about becoming another Pompeii, the Roman city covered by volcanic ash in A.D. 79.

Even in the worst eruption, deep ash deposits or lava flows should be confined to Mount Rainier National Park.

Like Californians shrugging off the next big earthquake, residents bet that 14,410-foot Mount Rainier won't erupt anytime soon.

David Babcock, 38, who owns a restaurant in Eatonville about 25 miles east of the mountain, says worrying is a waste of time.

"It's not a topic of conversation, other than people know it's going to blow one of these days," he says. "It's a question of when — not if."

Meg Vibbert, 62, who lives in the shadow of the majestic peak, says the view of Mount Rainier is worth the risk. "All I think about is its beauty," she says.

Mudflows from volcano could threaten the Seattle area

Areas at risk, should the Mount Rainier volcano erupt:

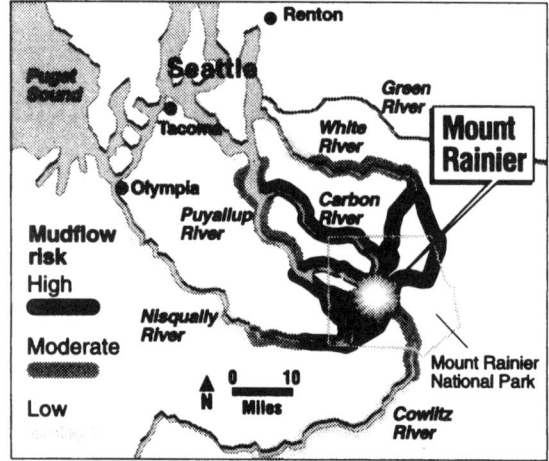

MENACING MOUNTAIN: With the Space Needle in the foreground, Mount Rainier looms large beyond the Seattle skyline.

Sources: National Research Council, *Mount Rainier: Active Cascade Volcano*

By Marty Baumann, USA TODAY

DISCOVERY FILE

Plate Tectonics and Volcanoes

The Plate Tectonics Theory

Plate tectonics sounds like it could be the upset stomach you can get by eating food from a dirty plate. But plate tectonics is actually a well-accepted theory about Earth's crust. Plate tectonics explains earthquakes and volcanoes. It also explains the existence of the highest mountains and the deepest trenches.

According to plate tectonics, Earth's surface is broken into a number of shifting slabs or plates. These plates average about 80 kilometers (50 miles) thick and move about on the hotter, deeper, and more mobile zone called the *mantle*. The Pacific plate travels the fastest. It moves at average rates of about 10 centimeters each year.

Most of the world's active volcanoes are found along or near the boundaries between these shifting plates. These are called *plate-boundary volcanoes*. Other active volcanoes are not found near plate boundaries; many of these intraplate volcanoes form almost straight chains of volcanic islands in the middle of some oceanic plates.

The Hawaiian Islands are perhaps the best example of an intraplate volcanic chain. This string of islands was formed as the Pacific plate moved in a northwesterly direction, passing over what scientists call a stationary "hot spot." Over the centuries, magma rising from the hot spot has built each of Hawaii's volcanoes.

On the margins of the Pacific Ocean basin, where the boundaries of several plates collide, many active and dormant volcanoes form what is termed the "Ring of Fire."

The Ring of Fire contains more than 75 percent of the 850 active volcanoes on Earth. Part of this ring runs along the west coast of the Americas from Chile to Alaska and includes Mount Rainier and Mount St. Helens in the Cascade Range of Washington and Oregon. It also extends down the east coast of Asia from Siberia to New Zealand—including Mount Pinatubo in the Philippines. Twenty percent of the Ring of Fire volcanoes are located in Indonesia. Other major groupings are found in Japan, the Aleutian Islands of Alaska, and Central America.

The Ring of Fire marks the boundary between the plates underlying the Pacific Ocean and the plates that make up the surrounding continents. Other volcanically active areas include the Mediterranean Sea and Iceland. Mediterranean volcanoes are found on the boundary where the African and Eurasian plates meet. The volcanoes that make up the still-growing island of Iceland are evidence that the Atlantic Ocean floor is spreading along the midoceanic ridge.

Where one tectonic plate meets another, a number of different things can happen:

1. The plates may be moving apart.
2. The plates may be pushing together.
3. One plate may be sliding past the other.

An example of plates moving apart is the Mid-Atlantic Ridge. The sea floor there is spreading apart at a rate up to 2.5 centimeters (1 inch) each year—about the rate your fingernails grow. Molten rock from

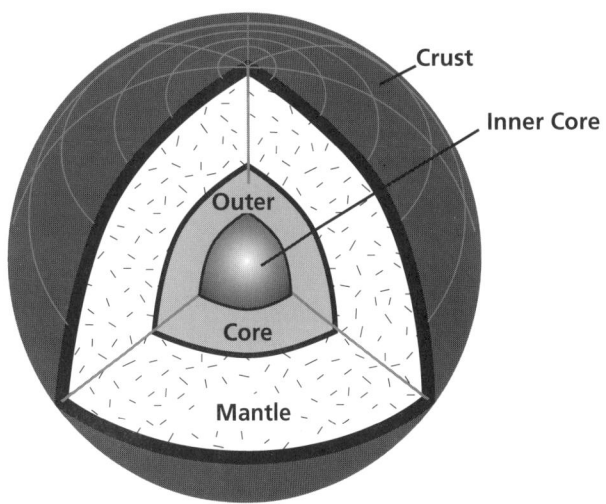

Cross-section of the Earth

Crust
Inner Core
Outer Core
Mantle

The Task 19

The Ring of Fire

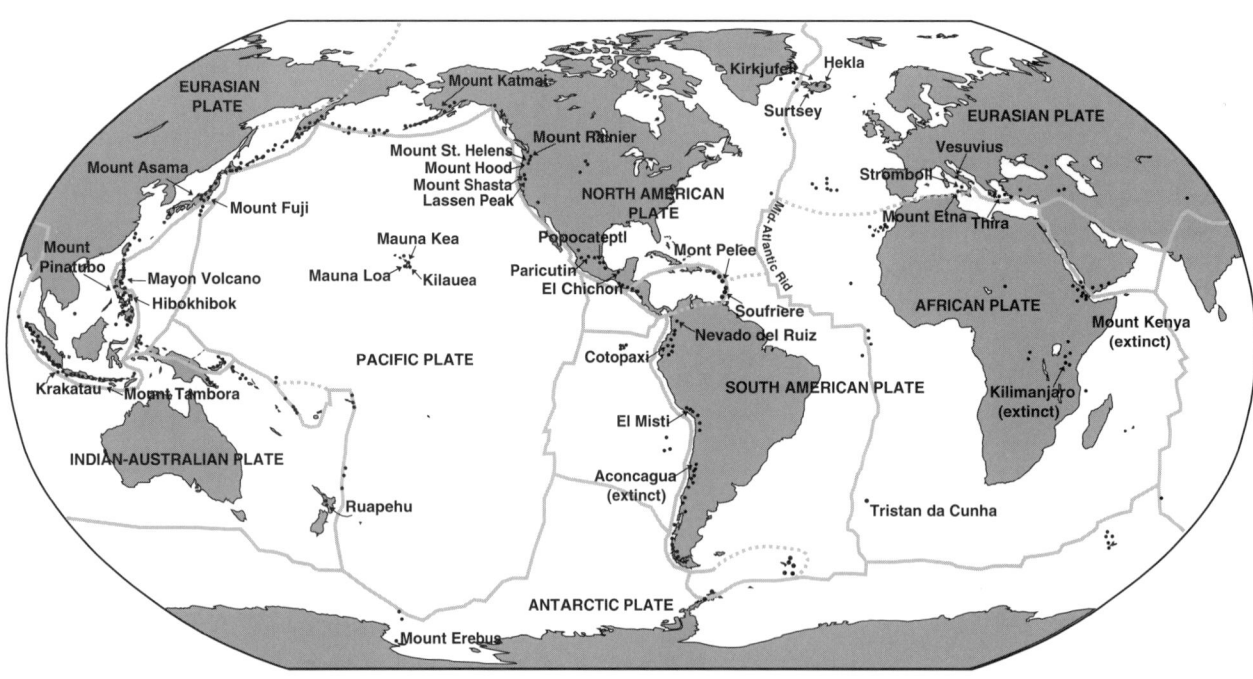

the mantle rises through cracks, creating new ocean floor. *Pillow lava* is one of the formations found here.

In other areas, ocean floor is being devoured. These *subduction zones* are deep oceanic trenches where the edges of denser, fast-moving plates plunge under less-mobile, less-dense plates. The deepest of these regions is the Mariana trench in the South Pacific near the island of Guam. Here, the Pacific plate dives under the less dense Eurasian plate. Can you find how deep the Mariana trench is?

The Ring of Fire is where we find many subduction zones.

When the relatively cool material of the oceanic crust is forced down into the hot mantle rock at the edge of a continent, it can cause earthquakes and volcanoes.

Earthquakes and Volcanoes

Although the movement of molten rock beneath an active volcano can cause earthquakes, generally these Earth tremors are relatively small. During violent eruptions, earthquakes can be locally severe, but they are usually not felt at long distances.

In early August 1959, about three months before the mid-November eruption of Hawaii's Kilauea, scientists reported a series of earthquakes coming from 35 miles below the islands. By the middle of September, these earthquakes were originating at depths of as little as half a mile. During the two months before the volcano erupted, seismographs recorded more than 22,000 earthquakes.

Changing depths and frequencies of earthquakes sometimes give scientists warning of impending eruptions.

Student Voices

We were forced to evacuate our home at Clark Air Base early in the morning with only an hour's notice. I never got to say good-bye to my friends or find out where they went, and my mom and I were separated from my father for eight months.

At first, I didn't take the warnings seriously. But after a while, I got more and more nervous. The night before the evacuation order came, I decided to pack my bags, even though my parents laughed at me for being too worried. The next day, the traffic jams were unbelievable, and it took forever to get off the base. There were thousands of cars on the road. The Air Force described it as one of the largest peacetime evacuations of this century. Until I moved to the Philippines with my family, I had never experienced a natural disaster. I now know how awesome the forces of nature can be and how they can suddenly turn your whole world upside down.

If I were part of your team, I would include lots of video of the volcano itself, especially during the eruption. Also, I would show scenes of the surrounding area before and after the eruption so people could understand how far-reaching the devastation can be. Include buildings collapsing under the weight of volcanic mud falling from the sky, show clogged roads, and show bridges washed away by the force of the mudflows. Then I would follow up with interviews with victims who lost everything they owned and show the vast scale of relief efforts needed to cope with the tragedy.

DAVID BAKER
AUSTIN, TX

IN THE NEWS

Volcanoes

Each volcano has its own temperament and timetable. Susan Russell-Robinson of the U.S. Geological Survey tells why volcanoes erupt, where and what to do when they do.

Q: Why after 600 years of no activity, did Mount Pinatubo in the Philippines erupt this week?

A: Volcanoes each have their own individual eruption style and time scale. This volcano probably has a time frame where it erupts in the order of every 500 to 1,000 years, versus a volcano like in Hawaii that seems to erupt every year, or some of the Alaskan volcanoes that might erupt every 10 or 20 years.

Q: So nothing triggered it?

A: There's nothing out of the ordinary about the fact that this volcano is erupting. If you were to take an ordinary calendar year, 50 to 75 to 80 volcanoes erupt around the world every year. There are 20 to 30 volcanoes every month that show signs of unrest. That might be a full-blown eruption, or increased seismic activity, or sudden steaming out vents for the volcano or a whole host of activities like that.

Q: What is the greatest thing to fear from a volcano?

A: In the case of a volcano that erupts explosively, the material that comes out is very, very hot. It carries toxic gasses and can move down slopes at speeds in excess of 125 miles per hour. You certainly can't outrun even a volcano like the Hawaiian volcanoes, where the lava is like a slow oozing molasses. On steep slopes it can move 30 miles per hour. So being caught in either type of eruption can be dangerous because you do have toxic gasses and the material is so hot it can exceed the human rate of movement.

Q: How does this eruption, which apparently spewed ash and smoke 50,000 feet high, compare to that of Mount St. Helens in Washington in 1980?

A: It had ash plumes that went as high as 90,000 feet. You're talking about plumes going up 12 to 18 miles

Even the Earth needs to let off steam once in a while

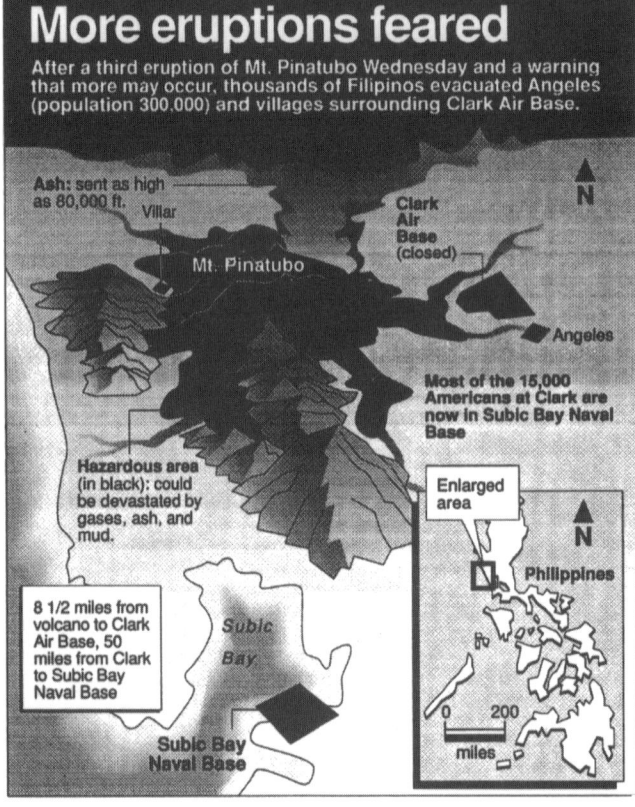

More eruptions feared
After a third eruption of Mt. Pinatubo Wednesday and a warning that more may occur, thousands of Filipinos evacuated Angeles (population 300,000) and villages surrounding Clark Air Base.

By Sam Ward, USA TODAY

and actually puncturing what we call the tropopause and went on into the stratosphere. A 50,000 foot high plume, though spectacular, is certainly not the greatest potential of a volcano.

Q: How high could one go?

A: If we look at the past 500 years, the largest eruption we know of was Tambora, Indonesia in 1815. That eruption was so large, there was so much ash in the atmosphere that the year of 1816 for North America and Europe was known as the year without a summer because the weather was significantly cooler as a result of that event.

Q: What is the 'ring of fire'?

A: If you look at where active volcanoes are placed around the world, there are somewhere between 500 and 600 of them. There is what appears to be almost a necklace that goes around the Pacific Ocean. If you start on the eastern side of the tip of South America and run along the west coast of South America, Central America, North America, down the Aleutian peninsula to the Soviet Union's Kamchatka peninsula down through Japan, on around through the Philippines to Indonesia, swing around the East side of Australia to New Zealand, you have a ring where something on the order of 60% of the world's volcanoes lie. It makes a ring around the Pacific.

Q: Why such a concentration there?

A: That's based on a theory we have called plate tectonics, that the ocean and the continents are like separate pieces. When they collide, one rides up over the other one. In this case, the Pacific Ocean goes under the continent and when that happens it seems to produce magma at depth and then you have volcanoes in the same ring, or you also have earthquakes.

Q: What part of the United States is part of the ring of fire?

A: The Western United States is. The volcano we know as the Cascade Range, for example, is part of that ring, as well as the whole Aleutian Chain, which is totally comprised of volcanoes. California, Oregon, Washington and Alaska have had eruptions within the last 100 years. Other states that have volcanic activity as recent as or during the last 10,000 years include Arizona, New Mexico, Utah, Nevada, Idaho.

Q: Is the volcano active in southern Japan right now part of the ring of fire?

A: There are many volcanoes that are active on that ring at the same time. It is just a coincidence that it erupted at the same time as Mount Pinatubo. In any given year, based on statistics the Smithsonian has been compiling, somewhere between 50 to 80 volcanoes erupt every year. The majority of them are on the ring of fire.

*Susan Russell-Robinson, 37, is a geologist and an information scientist at the U.S. Geological Survey in Reston, Va. The agency is a part of the Department of the Interior. She was interviewed by USA TODAY's **Barbara Reynolds**.*

The Story—Part 2

There She Blows!

The mountain appeared ready to become ground zero for Mother Nature at her worst—an energetic and highly destructive volcano. But should scientists call for a complete evacuation of the area? Could they rely on their data? What if their predictions were wrong, throwing people into unnecessary panic? About 300,000 people lived in and around the city of Angeles, which would be in the path of any volcanic debris flows. Should they be advised to flee?

Philippine and U.S. Geological Survey volcanologists decided it was time to evacuate. The Philippine government ordered the emergency evacuation of 20,000 people within six miles of Mount Pinatubo. Soon, about 55,000 people had fled.

At the U.S.-operated Clark Air Base, just seven miles southeast of Pinatubo, nearly 15,000 Americans were evacuated, including patients in a 200-bed hospital. Millions of dollars worth of equipment and aircraft had to be moved. Only essential personnel were left behind at the base to take advantage of the movie running at the base theater: *The Last Days of Pompeii*. Long lines of automobiles, packed with families from the air base and their belongings, snaked their way to the Subic Bay Naval Base, 50 miles to the south.

Seismic tremors continued to rattle the area, indicating the movement of magma. An eruption was imminent! Scientists declared a level 4 emergency on June 7 with the message, "Eruption possible within 24 hours." The government ordered everyone within a 12-mile radius of the volcano to evacuate.

Day and night, thousands of people from villages, the city of Angeles, and the air base streamed away from the impending eruption. Meanwhile, Mount Pinatubo continued to prepare itself, as it had done since May, for its first major outburst in more than 600 years. On June 12, gray ash billowed skyward about 20 kilometers (12.5 miles)—an explosive prelude to an even greater event to occur 48 hours later.

As the sun began to light the island skies on June 15, 1991, Mount Pinatubo unleashed its fury. Just before 6:00 A.M., a colossal eruption hurled huge amounts of ash and fiery debris upward. The blast tossed an ash cloud more than 19 kilometers (12 miles) high into the sky. The ash cloud quickly broadened to 16 kilometers (10 miles) wide. Earthquakes rippled across the landscape, demolishing several nearby unoccupied villages. Molten rocks tumbled down the lush northern and western slopes of the volcano. Scientists quickly issued a level-5 alert—an eruption had begun. ■

STUDENT VOICES

Just before the eruption, smoke was coming out and there were earthquakes one right after the other. The first eruption was loud. It came around noon. After that, it was pitch dark and smelled like rotten eggs. I really don't want to live near a volcano again, because I don't want to go through losing my friends again.

When you design your production, be sure to show how people were acting when the eruption was going on and what the Air Force did for them.

TANIA THORP
MIDWEST CITY, OK

Discovery File

Products of Eruptions:

Gas, Lava, Ash, and Volcanic Bombs

Volcanic Gases

When a volcano erupts, it releases gases, liquids, and solids. The gases contain a lot of carbon dioxide and steam from groundwater, but they also have hydrochloric acid (which burns your nose and throat), nasty sulfur compounds such as sulfur dioxide (the choking sulfur smell) or hydrogen sulfide (the rotten-eggs smell), and nitrogen.

The steam condenses in the air and forms clouds that produce heavy rain. The rain-soaked land can start sliding, becoming massive debris flows called *lahars*.

Water is a big factor in explosive eruptions because it can become "superheated" steam. Volcanic clouds rise and drift far beyond the volcano.

Types of Lava

Magma is gas-rich, molten (melted) rock beneath Earth's surface. When it erupts or escapes, it is called *lava*. Lava can have a wide variety of characteristics, depending on what it is made of.

There are many types of lava. The most common types are basalt and rhyolite. All lavas contain similar elements—silica (silicon dioxide) and oxides of calcium, sodium, aluminum, potassium, magnesium, and iron. Different proportions of these elements make very different lava.

You can group lava based on its silica content. Earth's most common volcanic rocks are *basalts*. They have less than 54 percent silica by weight. The lower the silica content, the less viscous and the more fluid the lava. Basalt lava can flow far from its source and spread out in a thin layer over large areas, creating shield volcanoes. Basalt lavas are typical of the volcanoes of Hawaii. They are rich in iron and magnesium. These elements give them their dark color.

The lava next lowest in silica is *andesite*. It has a silica content of between 54 to 62 percent. Andesite was named after the Andes Mountains of South America. Most composite volcanoes are built of layers of andesite.

Andesite forms many volcanoes in the Cascade Range of the Pacific Northwest. Mount Rainier and Mount Baker are almost entirely composed of pyroxene andesite, a name related to the mineral pyroxene that is abundant in this form of lava. Pyroxene andesite is usually dark gray or brown in color.

Lava with a silica content of 62 to 64 percent is called *dacite* (pronounced "day-site"). It is thick and pasty when molten. Mount St. Helens and Mount Mazama (Crater Lake) show a variety of chemical composition in their lavas. They erupt basalts and dacites as well as andesites.

In *rhyolite*, the silica content is 72 percent or more. Although generally light in color, some rhyolites and rhyodacites (silica 68 to 72 percent) are dark. The most stunning form of rhyolite is obsidian, a shiny, black volcanic glass. Along the Cascade Lakes Highway southwest of Bend, Oregon, there is a chain of rhyolite domes that sparkle in the sunlight.

In addition to the composition of lava, other factors can affect its speed and the formations it creates. Those other factors include the temperature and cooling rate, the amount of gas in the lava, and how quickly the gas escapes.

Forms of Basaltic Lava—A'a and Pahoehoe

The fluidity of a lava, or its resistance to flow, is called its *viscosity*. How much the molecules in a liquid rub together (friction) determines how slow it flows. The more friction a liquid has, the slower it flows. Viscosity is a major factor in what shapes lava-rock formations.

Hawaii's shield volcanoes are sometimes referred to as "drooling" volcanoes because their basaltic lava seeps from central craters as well as from small cones or fissures (cracks) on their sides.

Hawaiian volcanoes can also produce *fire fountains* that spew gas-rich lava high into the air. Most Hawaiian eruptions are quiet in contrast to the explosive eruptions characteristic of Mount St. Helens and Mount Pinatubo.

Because the Hawaiian volcanoes are excellent examples of

Volcano!

basaltic lava, the type of basalt lava flows have been given Hawaiian names—*pahoehoe* (pah-HOY-HOY) and *a'a* (AH-ah).

Pahoehoe has low viscosity and flows almost like water. In channels and on steep slopes, it can reach speeds of 16 to 24 kilometers (10 to 15 miles) per hour. This type of lava can flow great distances before it hardens, especially if it's rich in gas.

Pahoehoe has a smooth, billowy surface, often with a wrinkled or ropelike appearance where the "skin" that has started to form has been dragged along by the more fluid lava underneath. The rivers of pahoehoe quickly crust over but often leave streams of lava moving in tunnels underneath the crust.

When the supply of lava feeding the stream stops, the lava drains out, leaving an empty tunnel or lava tube. There is a 2,000-year-old lava tube near Mount St. Helens called Ape Cave. It is about four kilometers (2½ miles) long, and if you visit the national park there, you can walk through parts of this lava tube.

A'a is a slow-moving lava. Its surface is usually broken into angular, jagged fragments. Rock formed as a'a cools is shaped by gas spurting from the sluggish molten rock that is capped by a jagged, cooling crust. Thick, high-viscosity a'a moves very slowly, seldom more than 1½ kilometers (1 mile) an hour. You could walk faster than it flows. This sticky lava cools and hardens quickly, so it does not flow very far.

Fire Fountain, Pu'u O'o, Hawaii. By P. Mouginis-Mark, USGS

Most basaltic lava flows come out of a volcanic vent as pahoehoe and changes to the a'a form somewhere down the slope. The chemical composition of both kinds of lava is the same. Similar to a car, the lava slows down as it runs out of gas. The change occurs when a pahoehoe flow cools and loses some of its gas content. The number of crystals forming increases, and the flow starts to break up into jagged blocks, characteristic of a'a.

When lava flows into the sea, it cools fast and forms round masses that look like pillows. This is called *pillow lava*.

Volcanic Solids

Fragments of volcanic materials take on various forms as they are thrown out of a volcano. These fragments are called *pyroclasts*, from the Greek term meaning "fire broken."

Blocks are large angular chunks of solid rock. *Volcanic*

Pahoehoe lava flow, Hawaii. By P. Mouginis-Mark, USGS

Pahoehoe lava skin, Hawaii. By P. Mouginis-Mark, USGS

bombs are balls of molten lava that sometimes become pancake-flat when they plot on the ground. *Spindle bombs* are created as balls of molten lava twist through the air.

Cinder fragments that are hurled out from volcanoes are called *lapilli*, Latin for "little stone." Do you know the name of the volcanic rock that is light enough to float on water? It's called *pumice*. This porous rock is formed from glassy lava-foam blown from a vent. The gas-formed cavities left behind as the lava cools cause pumice to be buoyant. After Krakatau's eruption in 1883, rafts of pumice were found floating on the sea.

Ignimbrite is made of glassy fragments that are hot enough to weld together. Rich in silica, ignimbrite is formed when a lot of pumice erupts at extremely high temperatures.

Another volcanic phenomenon found in Hawaii is *Pele's hair*. It was named after the Hawaiian fire goddess, Pele, and is formed by small drops of runny lava flying through the air. The drops stretch out into thin threads of volcanic glass. They are found in clumps that look very much like hair.

A´a lava flow, Hawaii.

Volcanoes can spew out huge clouds of volcanic ash—tiny lava particles almost as fine as flour, or dust. It isn't really ash because it hasn't been burned. It's more like volcanic sand.

Ash and other rock debris often mix with heavy rain to produce destructive debris flows that can reach speeds of 48 kilometers (30 miles) per hour. Such a debris flow buried the Roman town of Herculaneum when Mount Vesuvius erupted in 79 A.D. If Mount Rainier becomes active, debris flows will be one of the greatest threats to people living in the surrounding valleys. Giant volcanic explosions can blanket land for miles around as they hurl gritty dust high into the atmosphere. As the dust settles down through the atmosphere and falls into the oceans, it adds layers to deep ocean sediments.

Although violent volcanic eruptions can destroy towns and farms, volcanic ash contains material that enriches soil and yields more productive crop growth.

Boulder Field, Halemaumau Crater, Hawaii.

A´a topography.

26   Volcano!

SCIENCE ACTIVITY

Through Thick and Thin

Purpose
To create a demonstration that will show how the composition of a liquid affects its viscosity.

Background
While researching volcanoes, you have come across some interesting information about magma. Magma is formed when large masses of rock deep below the surface become so hot they melt. When magma solidifies, it forms intrusive igneous rock. Two important Earth processes are listed below.

1. Rock melts to form magma.
2. New rock forms when magma solidifies.

Magma that flows from the ground and over Earth's surface is called *lava*. Lava is igneous rock that has been formed on the earth's surface. By observing the behavior of lava, scientists have learned much about the compositions, temperatures, and liquid properties of different types of magmas. They have learned that not all lava flows at the same speed. Some of the lava at Mauna Loa in Hawaii has reached speeds of 16 kilometers per hour, but most lava flow rates are measured in meters per hour or meters per day!

Viscosity is a property of liquids used to describe resistance to flow. During your research, you may have learned that the viscosity of a magma depends on temperature and composition. The key component that determines the viscosity of magma is silica. You have seen crystals of silica before. It forms the very common mineral called *quartz*. Silica is also the main component in synthetically produced glass. The more silica crystals contained in a magma, the greater its viscosity.

Since your contract with the state requires at least one demonstration, your project coordinator has suggested you develop one that will help explain viscosity and its relationship to lava flow.

Materials
For each pair:
- Water
- 100 ml or more heavy corn syrup
- 100 ml or more rubbing alcohol
- 100 ml or more glycerin
- 100 ml or more cooking oil
- At least two 100-ml graduated cylinders
- Several small, round plastic beads
- Stopwatch
- Warm, soapy water and towels for cleanup

Procedure
Your project coordinator (teacher) has suggested you start the demonstration with a comparison of how long it takes a plastic bead to fall through two different substances. After you conduct trials, you can mix together different volumes of liquids to determine how various ratios of each affect the settling rate of a plastic bead released below the surface.

The coordinator wants you to keep accurate records of volumes (in milliliters) and time (in seconds). You should also calculate and keep a record of the concentrations of the solutions you test. For example, a solution made with 20 ml of corn syrup and 60 ml of water would have a concentration of 25 percent. The formula for the calculation of concentration is

concentration (%) = volume of test substance/total volume of solution x 100

or

$$\% = \frac{V_{test}}{V_{total}} \times 100$$

After you have tested various concentrations of syrup, water, and rubbing alcohol, you can test concentrations of other liquids.

How do you think changing the temperature of the solutions you tested would affect their viscosity? Check with your project coordinator and test your ideas, if possible.

Conclusion
After completing your experiment, prepare graphs that will make it easy for people to compare the viscosities of the solutions you tested.

Optional Homework (Extra Credit)
It's very late in the afternoon, and you are getting ready to go home for the evening. Your project coordinator calls you and tells you the class needs a good demonstration of how silica can thicken a magma. You

▶ continued on page 28

▶ continued from page 27

have until tomorrow morning to come up with a demonstration. The coordinator suggests the following experiment. (Do this activity at home under parental supervision.)

Materials
- Saucepan
- Spoon
- 1 ¼ C water
- 2 T cornstarch

Procedure
1. Boil 1 cup of water in the saucepan.
2. Mix 2 tablespoons cornstarch in ¼ cup water. Stir well to mix.
3. Slowly add the cornstarch-water mixture to the boiling water. Boil for about two minutes.
4. Remove the pan from the stove and let it cool.
5. Decide how this experiment relates to the statement above and write your report.

Discovery File

Geysers and Smokers

Geysers and other similar vents are plentiful in certain areas of the United States, Iceland, Italy, and New Zealand. They squirt, spray, or dribble steamy water, gas, and mud heated by volcanoes nearing extinction. Here are brief descriptions of some interesting volcano-related phenomena.

1. **Hot springs** are springs whose water is heated by hot rocks underground. Hot springs often deposit dissolved minerals at their edges, producing crusts of *travertine* (calcium carbonate) or *geyserite* (quartz). Mineral deposits can create stepped formations known as *sinter terraces*, such as those in Mammoth Hot Springs in Yellowstone National Park. Other famous hot springs occur in Iceland, and on New Zealand's North Island.
2. **Smokers** are hot springs on a spreading ridge on the ocean's floor. When sulfides (compounds of sulfur and a metallic element) are spewed into hot water, they build mineral chimneys that vent black, smoky clouds. Some well-known smokers are on the Galápagos Rise.
3. **Geysers** are periodic fountains of steam and hot water. The best known of the many geysers in Yellowstone National Park is the world-famous geyser, Old Faithful. The fountains are driven up from deep below the surface when water becomes superheated. Other well-known geysers can be found in Iceland.

Old Faithful Geyser, Yellowstone National Park — PhotoDisc

4. **Mud volcanoes** are mud-rich waters vented from below the surface, creating low mud cones. Examples are found in Iceland, New Zealand's North Island, and Sicily.
5. **Fumaroles** are small vents that discharge jets of steam. You can find active fumaroles at Mount Etna, Sicily. Alaska's Valley of Ten Thousand Smokes gave up smoking after a very active period in the early 1900s.
6. **Solfataras** are a type of volcanic vent that emits steam and sulfurous gas. They take their name from one near Naples, Italy.
7. **Mofettes** are gases laced with carbon dioxide. They are expelled from small vents. Examples occur in France, Italy, and Java.

Discovery File

Danger! Pyroclastic Flows

Streams of hot ash and rock fragments mixed with hot air and other gases roar down the side of a volcano. These are called *pyroclastic flows*. They move along the surface just like flowing water, yet these flows are hot and dry.

Pyroclastic flows are spectacular events caused by volcanic activity. They can be formed when masses of hot ash and rock fragments are tossed into the air above a vent and then fall back onto the sides of a volcano and flow downhill. Pyroclastic flows are also born when gas-rich lava froths in the throat of the volcano and pours out of the crater as a mixture of hot ash and gas. They are also formed when a large mass of rock, consisting of a hot mixture of rock fragments and air, avalanches down the side of a growing volcanic dome.

Pyroclastic flows are accompanied by clouds of ash that billow hundreds or even thousands of feet into the air above and beyond the flow itself. Pyroclastic flows often extend many miles from the volcano. These flows are very dangerous: they can reach speeds of more than 100 miles per hour. Because of their high temperatures—hotter than boiling water—pyroclastic flows can set fire to vegetation and wooden structures in their paths.

One type of pyroclastic flow is called an *ash hurricane*. This is a cloudlike mass of hot ash and gas that rushes at high speed over hills and ridges and down valley floors. Formed in much the same way as other pyroclastic flows, ash hurricanes carry mostly sand-sized material.

Pyroclastic flows and ash hurricanes are extremely dangerous. They move so fast that escape from these blasts is nearly impossible; they can burn and suffocate people who find themselves in their lethal paths.

By Richard Hoblitt, USGS

SCIENCE ACTIVITY

Here Comes the Mud

Purpose
To estimate the time available to evacuate three communities in a valley below Mount Rainier if a mudflow is on its way.

Background
About 500 years ago, around the time Columbus arrived in North America, a mudflow swept down the slopes of Mount Rainier. It followed the Puyallup River valley, covering the land with thick, hot mud. Today, the towns of Auburn, Sumner, and Orting lie in the path of a similar mudflow. Thousands of lives are at risk.

What caused the mudflow 500 years ago? No geological evidence indicates that a volcanic eruption caused it. Could such a mudflow happen again in this valley?

An automated system is being planned that will monitor the slopes of Mount Rainier for mudflows and immediately alert the residents below. You are a geological engineer for the state of Washington. You have been asked to estimate the time from the sounding of a mudflow alert to the actual arrival of the mud. This is the amount of time that will be available to evacuate the 5,000 residents of each of these communities once a warning is sounded.

Materials
For each student:
- Road map of Mount Rainier area
- Metric ruler

Procedure
You have decided to prepare best-case and worst-case estimates based on your knowledge of past mudflows. In the best case, the mud will travel at a speed of 10 kilometers per hour. In the worst case, the mud will flow at a speed of 50 kilometers per hour.

Use the highway map below to measure distances.

Conclusion
After completing your calculations, prepare a brief memo to the governor. Give the governor your best- and worst-case estimates. Think about the questions below as you prepare your memo and comment on your answers to them and your reasons for your answers.

1. Should city and county officials prepare evacuation plans?
2. Should the communities prepare escape routes up nearby valley walls?
3. How might the weather or time of day affect an evacuation?
4. Would an evacuation plan affect the value of property?
5. Where should schools be built in the future?
6. Could any structures be built to avert a mudflow?

30   *Volcano!*

Discovery File

Volcano Hazards Facts Sheet

GLACIER-GENERATED DEBRIS FLOWS AT MOUNT RAINIER

Mount Rainier is a young volcano whose slopes are undergoing rapid change by a variety of geologic processes, including debris flows. Debris flows are churning masses of water, rock and mud that travel rapidly down the volcano's steep, glacially carved valleys, leaving in their wake splintered trees, picnic sites buried in mud, and damaged roads. Debris flows typically contain as much as 65 to 70 percent rock and soil by volume and have the appearance of wet concrete. At Mount Rainier National Park, these flows invariably begin in remote areas nearly inaccessible to people, but may move rapidly downstream into areas frequently by visitors.

The smallest, but most frequent, debris flows at Mount Rainier begin as glacial outburst floods, also called by the Icelandic term "jökulhlaup" (pronounced "yo-kul-hloip"). Outburst floods at Mount Rainier form from sudden release of water stored at the base of glaciers or within the glacier ice. Outburst floods have been recorded from four glaciers on Mount Rainier: the Nisqually, Kautz, South Tahoma, and Winthrop glaciers. From 1986 through 1992, South Tahoma Glacier released a total of 15 outburst floods, including at least one every year. These outburst floods from South Tahoma Glacier occurred during periods of unusually hot or rainy weather in summer or early autumn, and were apparently caused by rapid input of meltwater or rainwater to the base of the glacier. The exact timing of such outburst floods is unpredictable, however.

Outburst floods become debris flows by incorporating large quantities of sediment from valley floors and walls, often triggering landslides that mix with the flood waters. The transformation from water flood to debris flow occurs in areas where streams have eroded glacially derived sediments and sediment-rich, stagnant glacier ice that was stranded in valleys as glaciers thinned and retreated earlier in this century. As the stagnant ice melts over the next several decades, it will release its charge of sediment into the stream valleys. That sediment will potentially be incorporated into more debris flows if it is mobilized by outburst floods.

Glacier-generated debris flows at Mt. Rainier travel downstream at speeds of 5-10 meters per second (10-20 miles per hour) or more. People who have witnessed them report that only 1-2 minutes may pass between the time the roaring sound of an approaching debris flow is heard and the time the flow rushes past. These flows typically have steep, bouldery snouts--up to 10-20 meters (30-60 feet) high in the most constricted parts of a stream valley--followed by a churning mass of mud, rock, and vegetation. Their deafening noise is often accompanied by strong local wind, thick dust clouds, and violent ground shaking.

Debris flows usually follow stream channels and construct their own levees as they move, but their exact paths are unpredictable. As a debris flow moves downstream from Mount Rainier's steep flanks onto relatively gentle slopes, the flow's bouldery snout may clog the stream channel; the moving mass behind the snout may then overtop the banks and cut a new channel, perhaps through forest or across trails and roads. Debris flows at Mount Rainier typically come to rest after perhaps 30 minutes to an hour, leaving muddy, bouldery deposits from which muddy water drains for a period of a few hours to a few days. Near the valley mouth, however, the only hint of the havoc upstream might be a small increase in water level and a change in the stream's color to a murky brown or gray.

The largest debris flows at Mount Rainier are unrelated to glacial outburst floods. Several times during the last 6,000 years, debris flows enormously larger than any caused by outburst floods were triggered by huge rock avalanches and travelled far beyond the park boundaries. See the reports by Crandell and by Scott and others (cited on the other side of this sheet) for discussion of potential hazards of these giant debris flows.

Visitors can see effects of recent glacier-generated debris flows at the following sites:

KAUTZ CREEK—The largest debris flow since the establishment of the park occurred October 2-3, 1947, when heavy rains apparently triggered an outburst flood from Kautz Glacier. The flood passed over the lowest part of the glacier, eroding a gorge through the ice, then mobilized sediment and transformed into a debris flow as it continued downvalley. Nine kilometers (5.5 miles) downstream from the glacier, the Nisqually-Longmire Road (equivalent to Highway 706 west of the park entrance) was buried by 9 meters (28 feet) of mud and debris. About 40 million cubic meters (50 million

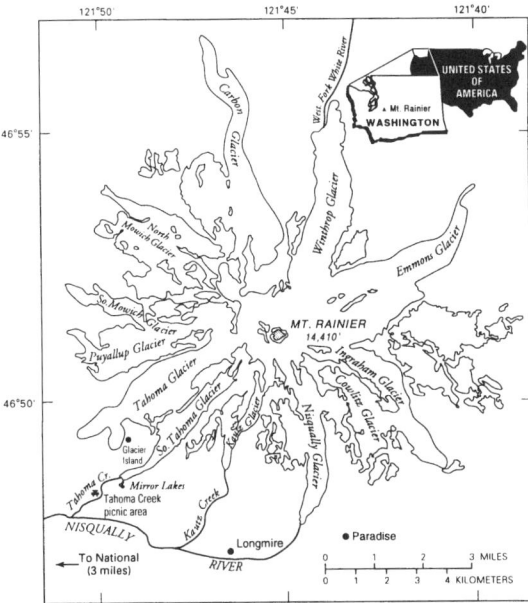

Schematic diagram of major glaciers on Mount Rainier

cubic yards) of sediment were moved, including boulders up to 4 meters (13 feet) in diameter. Although Kautz Creek has subsequently cut down through those deposits, visitors to the park will notice that they are driving uphill as they approach the creek. To observe deposits of the 1947 debris flow, along with upright dead trees buried by those deposits, stop at the parking lot on the east side of Kautz Creek. Smaller debris flows have moved along Kautz Creek in 1961, 1985, 1986, and perhaps at other times.

From Longmire, hike the Wonderland Trail about 3 kilometers (2 miles) to where it crosses Kautz Creek. Boulders strewn across the valley there were deposited by the 1947 debris flow. Note the splintered trees that lined a former stream channel, and trees that lie buried horizontally in older debris-flow deposits. Above the boulder-strewn region and amid the forest lie moss-covered logs downed by previous debris flows.

NISQUALLY RIVER—Debris flows triggered by outburst floods from Nisqually Glacier damaged or destroyed bridges over the Nisqually River in 1926, 1932, 1934, and 1955. The present bridge has not been damaged by subsequent floods, which occurred in 1968, 1970, 1972, 1985, and perhaps on other occasions.

At the Glacier Bridge over the Nisqually River, observe the boulder berms constructed by debris flows in the 1930's and 1950's. Twisted reinforcing bar and weathered concrete are all that remain of the 1930's-vintage bridge foundation about 100 meters (110 yards) upstream.

TAHOMA CREEK—At least 23 debris flows triggered by outburst floods from South Tahoma Glacier have moved down Tahoma Creek since 1967. These flows have carved a gorge as much as 40 meters (130 feet) deep into sediment and stagnant ice below the terminus of South Tahoma Glacier. The hazard of potential debris flows has prompted the National Park Service to close the Westside Road to visitors' automobiles at a point about 4 kilometers (2.5 miles) from the junction with the Nisqually-Longmire Road. Bouldery debris-flow deposits have buried the Westside Road about 600 meters (660 yards) farther upstream, near the confluence of Tahoma Creek and Fish Creek, on several occasions since 1988. In the vicinity of a former picnic area, about 1.6 kilometers (1 mile) beyond the road closure, bouldery deposits have accumulated at the extremely rapid rate of nearly 0.5 meters per year (1.5 feet per year) since 1988. About 1 kilometer (0.6 miles) of the Tahoma Creek hiking trail, which began at the picnic area, has been obliterated, and the forest has been badly damaged.

South Tahoma Glacier and the uppermost reach of Tahoma Creek, including the gorge eroded by recent debris flows, are visible from Mirror Lakes, near Indian Henry's Hunting Ground. The lowermost part of the gorge is crossed by the Wonderland Trail suspension bridge at a point about 3 kilometers (2 miles) upstream of the destroyed picnic area. Erosion by passing debris flows has deepened the gorge beneath the bridge from 10 meters (30 feet) to 25 meters (80 feet) since 1986.

PRECAUTIONS FOR VISITORS

Because outburst floods are unpredictable, you should be alert when visiting valleys with glacier-fed streams, particularly on unusually hot or rainy days. If you are near a stream and hear a roaring sound coming from upvalley, or note a rapid rise in water level, move quickly up the stream embankment, away from the stream channel and to higher ground. Do not try to escape by moving downstream; debris flows move faster than you can run. Observe Park Service regulations, especially those provided for your safety in areas prone to debris flows. Here, as in most areas in other national parks, natural processes such as floods and debris flows are allowed to occur without human intervention.

FURTHER READING

Crandell, D.R., 1969, The geologic story of Mount Rainier: U.S. Geological Survey Bulletin 1292, 43 p.

---1971, Postglacial lahars from Mount Rainier Volcano, Washington: U.S. Geological Survey Professional Paper 677, 75 p.

Driedger, C.L., 1986, A visitor's guide to Mount Rainier glaciers: Longmire, Washington, Pacific Northwest National Parks and Forests Association, 80 p.

Scott, K.M., Pringle, P.T., and Vallance, J.W., 1992, Sedimentology, behavior and hazards of debris flows at Mount Rainier, Washington: U.S. Geological Survey Open-file Report 90-385, 106 p.

Walder, J.S., and Driedger, C.L., 1994, Geomorphic drainage caused by outburst floods and debris flows at Mount Rainier, Washington, with emphasis on Tahoma Creek Valley: U.S. Geological Survey, Water-Resources Investigations Report 93-4093, 93 p.

Debris flow at Tahoma Creek, July 26, 1988
Photograph by G.G. Parker

— Joseph S. Walder and Carolyn L. Driedger

For additional information, contact:
U.S. Geological Survey
Cascades Volcano Observatory
5400 MacArthur Boulevard
Vancouver, Washington 98661
Telephone (206) 696-7693   FAX (206) 696-7866
E-mail: cvo@pwavan.wr.usgs.gov
Internet: http://vulcan.wr.usgs.gov/

July 1993 (Reprinted August 1995)   Open-File Report 93-124 (Replaces Open-File Report 91-242)

ON THE JOB

Geological Engineer

DR. MEGHAN MORRISSEY
U.S. GEOLOGICAL SURVEY
MENLO PARK, CA

I always liked science as a child, and I particularly liked being out-of-doors, but when I was your age, I never dreamed that one day I would be a scientist studying volcanoes. I still like watching nature shows on television and daydreaming about being in those places.

I work with the U.S. Geological Survey studying the earthquakes associated with volcanic activity. The focus of my research and analysis is the fluid dynamics inside volcanoes—how rising magma in a volcano creates earthquakes.

My master's degree is in geological engineering, and I earned a doctorate degree in geology. After receiving my geological engineering degree, I was headed for an environmental career, such as work in groundwater pollution. Then I took a class on volcanoes. It inspired me to continue my education and pursue a career in volcanology.

In that one class, I realized I'd found a niche for my interests. It was the mystery attached to volcanoes—so much hadn't been studied thoroughly—that attracted me. Now I'm applying what I've learned in geological engineering to understanding the dynamic processes taking place inside volcanoes.

My work allows me to travel to volcanoes in very exotic places such as South America and Iceland. Currently, I'm working on a computer simulation: I'm trying to reproduce earthquakes from known dynamic processes inside the volcanoes. Each day I come to work wanting to make a big step toward understanding what these earthquakes are telling us about volcanoes.

Earthquakes caused by volcanic activity are related to the movement of magma in the earth. One type of earthquake I study is associated with movement along fractures. Another type of earthquake is caused by gases flowing through these cracks toward the surface.

My goal is to bring about a whole new way of looking at volcanoes. Some people study volcanic gases, lava, pyroclastic flows, or geochemistry. I'm trying to integrate all of that into the big picture to understand the role of seismic activity and the dynamics of fluids as they move through a volcano.

I believe we must take a multidisciplinary look at volcanoes. That means getting scientists in the various disciplines talking to each other. You can't just focus on one aspect of volcanoes. To get the larger picture, you have to collaborate and work together. If you like to work with other people, science is the way to go.

When you're close to a volcano, you appreciate its beauty and its power. When you walk on one, you feel the heat, and you see the deformation going on and the gases spewing out. You realize that the earth is not just a passive, solid body. It's alive, and we're like ants on top of a moving ant hill. We have to learn to live with nature. Volcanoes are an awesome part of it all. The more we can learn about volcanoes and other earth processes, the better off we're going to be.

Volcanoes can be very dangerous, and we aren't always able to predict eruptions. In January 1993, I was doing research at the

Galeras volcano in Colombia, South America. It was my first field trip to a volcano. I was in a car on the lower slopes of Galeras when there was a surprise eruption. Columns of ash shot into the air and pumice and rocks flew out.

At first, I was very excited. I remember thinking, "Wow, it's erupting and I want to go up there." But then I remembered that people were already up there, and I was worried about them. Six volcanologists and three tourists were killed that day. Some people who were standing by the volcano's rim were cut up and badly burned by large blocks of lava.

Earlier that same morning, I had been walking around on that rim. Two days earlier, I had been down in the same vents where those people had been killed. That was unnerving. It could have happened to me. It taught me that volcanoes are dangerous: they are real, they are big, and they are something we can't control.

My advice on making a television program about Mount Rainier is to explain the events that warn of an eruption. Talk about the earthquakes that would take place. Show how seismic activity is telling us about the movement of magma deep within the volcano.

If I were on your team, I'd also include a look at the type of volcano Mount Rainier is. Would a Mount Rainier eruption be like a Mount St. Helens eruption, or more like another type of volcano? On what sides of the volcano would the *lahars* (mudflows) slide down? How would the local government react and to what extent would the eruption affect surrounding communities? How long would you wait before warning local people about a possible eruption? These are the questions I would like to see answered in the television program.

Remember, there is still a lot to explore about volcanoes. If you're interested in this field, take a lot of classes in general science as well as earth science. If you want to make a contribution to science or any other field you select, you have to put in the time and effort. Keep your eyes open and pay attention. Find something you like to do and work toward a goal.

The Story—Part 3

The Fall of Mount Pinatubo

A mushroom-shaped cloud of searing gas and ash around Mount Pinatubo blocked out the sun. An estimated 2 billion tons of pumice, ash, stones, and pebbles were thrown into the air from the bowels of the volcano. Slowly volcanic ash started to fall from the sky like dirty snow. People fleeing the scene used umbrellas to guard against falling volcanic debris. Most clutched handkerchiefs or scarves to their faces, trying to block the stench from sulfur fumes. Even the capital city of Manila, 60 miles away, was touched by falling ash. In Manila, as many as 150,000 sought shelter from the falling ash.

The commanding general of Clark Air Base ordered the last few people from the U.S. military installation to leave. The general later recalled that it didn't take seismic instruments or satellite data to know it was time to leave. Instead, he took the advice of someone running by: "General, you'd better put jam in your pockets, because we're all about to be toast."

Great masses of hot steam, rocks, and other material, called *pyroclastic flows*, churned out of Mount Pinatubo and rushed down its slopes. The climactic phase of the major eruption—one of the largest volcanic eruptions of the century—lasted more than 15 hours. It was later called "Black Saturday"—a time of darkness that stretched for 36 hours. Along with a black blizzard of coarse ash, Pinatubo's eruption caused claps of thunder, brilliant flashes of lightning, orange fireballs, and dozens of earthquakes.

But the worst was yet to come.

A set of tropical storms also hit the Philippines on June 15. The torrents of rain mixed with volcanic debris. The forests had been blown off the mountain, so there was nothing to hold waterlogged soil on the steep slopes. Mudflows and landslides plunged down the sides of Mount Pinatubo. The storms hampered evacuation and roads became clogged with ash and mud.

A blanket of volcanic ash one to two meters thick, made even heavier by the rain, covered buildings. Homes and buildings collapsed from the combination of the heavy ash and earthquakes. Clark Air Base alone lost 150 buildings. The base was later abandoned because of the destruction.

Volcanic ash was carried many miles by the strong winds of typhoon Yunya. Heavy ash fall even caused 11 commercial aircraft emergencies. As far away as 600 miles southwest of the volcano, airplane engines were

STUDENT VOICES

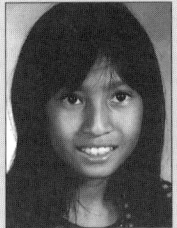

When Pinatubo first erupted, there was this big, huge cloud that looked like a mushroom. Then it started raining ashes that looked and felt like sand. The ashes smelled like fireworks. It sounded like sand pouring down hard. And there was a big earthquake that shook the whole house.

When you make your television show, make sure you use some evacuation footage. We had to wait in very long lines to get water, and we had to eat MRE's (meals ready to eat) until they ran out.

DANA BUENO
CONVERSE, TX

IN THE NEWS

Base escapes volcano's worst

Eruptions pose threat to air traffic

By Juan J. Walte
USA TODAY

Molten rock and boiling mud from new eruptions Wednesday of Mount Pinatubo volcano in the Philippines missed the Air Force's huge, and nearly vacant, Clark Air Base.

"Clark did not get any significant amount of ash or dust. There was no damage," said Pentagon spokesman Lt. Cmdr. Ned Lundquist.

While Filipinos living near the base grabbed their belongings and fled to safer ground, hundreds of U.S. Marines keeping watch at Clark, rode out the eruptions — the first by Pinatubo in 611 years.

Only one death has been reported. A Filipino serving in the U.S. Navy was killed when his car skidded on an ash-slickened road and crashed into a bus.

The eruptions' smoky plume was visible in Manila, 60 miles to the south. Stones the size of a man's head rained down.

The half dozen eruptions forced the evacuation of 600 of the 1,500 Marines and other troops left at Clark after more than 14,500 troops and their families fled two days earlier to Subic Bay Naval Base, 50 miles away.

The eruptions threaten to disrupt air traffic between the USA and Asia as airlines rerouted around the plume.

In the past, airliners that have hit dense volcanic clouds lost power, suddenly dived or sustained cracked windows, but none crashed, said Tom Casadevall of the U.S. Geological Survey.

"We are closely tracking the cloud," said United Airlines' Sarah Dornicker.

Meanwhile, at Subic Bay Naval Base, the people from Clark are coping fairly well under the circumstances. But, Lundquist said: "There's a lot of stress on everyone because you have a situation involving a base already at 100% capacity now doubling its population."

It's not clear how long they will stay at Subic Bay. U.S. Ambassador Nicholas Platt said Philippine seismologists advised him "it could be months before we know whether the danger is past."

Philippine volcano expert Delfin Garcia said the volcano was entering "an episode of big eruptions" that would continue indefinitely.

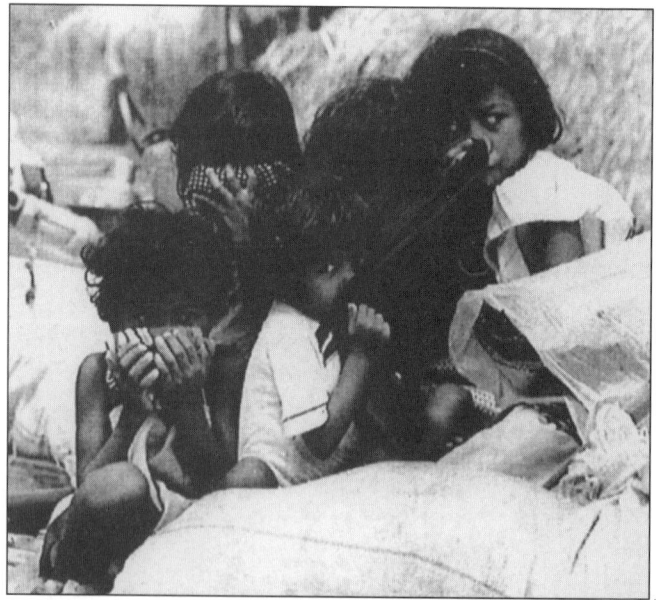

EVACUEES: Filipino children cover their noses as they ride a cart laden with their belongings. They are fleeing Mount Pinatubo volcano, which erupted three times Wednesday.
By Pat Roque, AP
JUNE 13, 1991

destroyed when they sucked in the gritty volcanic material.

Weather cleared long enough on June 16 to allow the first view of the volcano since the eruption. Pinatubo's top was gone, replaced by a depression more than a mile wide. Pyroclastic flow deposits filled a number of the valleys around the volcano. Scientists later calculated that up to 90 percent of Mount Pinatubo's top was transformed into avalanches of molten rock, gas, and ash.

More rain fell, causing hot mudflows to bury parts of some towns east of the volcano. Drainage patterns of rivers were altered by volcanic ash deposits and by mudflows.

Even in mid-August, two months after the eruption, thousands of people were forced to flee towns in the Pampanga and Tarlac regions because of threatening mudflows. Mudflows 16 feet deep wiped out main bridges across rivers and damaged countless homes. Central highways in the region were buried by avalanches that cascaded down the slopes of Mount Pinatubo during monsoon rains.

In total, the Pinatubo event left more than 200,000 people homeless. More than 720 people were killed, many of whom were caught in collapsing buildings or mudflows. Hundreds of people who were forced to live in tent cities and evacuation camps died due to illnesses. It was estimated that upwards of 650,000 people lost their jobs because of the Mount Pinatubo eruption. More than 108,000 houses were destroyed or damaged.

Although there were many tragedies resulting from the eruption of Mount Pinatubo, an even greater disaster was averted. Loss of life was low, despite the horrendous eruption. More than 80,000 people were successfully evacuated as the result of scientists' early warnings. ∎

SCIENCE ACTIVITY

The Fax and Nothing but the Fax

Purpose
To classify and identify igneous rocks.

Background
A geologist has donated igneous rock samples to your team for your television show. The geologist said the rocks would be labeled, and an identification key that explains how each rock was formed would come with the samples of rocks.

A heavy box of rocks arrives in the mail. Your coordinator tells you to see what you can do with them, so you open the box to get started. The samples look great, but there are no labels. At first, you don't think this will be a problem; you can use the key to identify the rocks. But as you dig through the box to find the identification key, no luck. The key and the rock labels have both been forgotten. "Now what?" you ask the coordinator. "Do the best you can," the coordinator says. "I'll try to have the key faxed to you. Good luck!"

Materials
For each pair:
- Unknown rocks in a box
- Hand lens
- Masking tape for labels
- Pen

Procedure
You're running out of time, so you've decided to try developing some type of classification system to help you make sense out of the rock samples you received.
- Study the samples and create a list of criteria that you can use to sort the samples into logical groups.
- Draw a table that shows your criteria, and use it to separate the samples into groups. Use masking tape to number the samples. Numbers will help you keep track of the samples. (You can also use the numbers on the table you develop.)
- After you finish, be sure to make a permanent record of the rocks that belong in each group and the criteria you used to separate the groups.
- Ask the project coordinator (your teacher) whether the fax has arrived and follow his or her directions.

Conclusion
1. Compare your classification system to one in a science book. How are they the same? How are they different? What changes would you make (in either)?
2. After completing the activity, write a letter to Dr. Sid A. Mentry and Mr. Matt O'Morfic thanking them for their interest in the program and the samples. Briefly explain the classification system you devised and how it compares to the classification system actually used for intrusive and extrusive rocks. Include an explanation of how you plan to use information about igneous rocks in the program.

IN THE NEWS

Mount Pinatubo blows

A volcano erupts when an ocean plate is pushed beneath a continental plate. Magma (melted rock inside the earth) then rises toward the surface and collects in the magma chamber. The molten rock becomes lighter and forces its way upward through the main vent, spewing lava, gases and ash.

Source: World Book — By Keith Carter, USA TODAY

At Subic, squeezed but safe

By Steve Marshall
USA TODAY

The 14,500 troops, spouses, children, dogs, cats and guinea pigs of Clark Air Base are 50 miles away at the Subic Bay Naval Base in the Philippines today. They are cramped, confused, broke, worried and disorganized — but safe from erupting Mount Pinatubo.

Hundreds of evacuees lined up at a makeshift Subic Bay center to collect advance pay. They had to flee the volcano so quickly there was no time to get to the bank.

Tuesday, the volcano, 8½ miles from Clark, was rocked by a huge explosion, and the remaining 1,500 personnel fled.

"We were notified four hours before evacuation," said Thelma Corpuz, as her husband Staff Sgt. Gil Corpuz of Wellesley, Calif., waited for his pay. "The banks were closed. We just grabbed what we needed, like a toothbrush."

Navy families were asked to accept "guests" from Clark, but there are only about 2,200 family housing units, not enough to absorb the influx.

So every nook and cranny of the base, from the chapel to recreation huts at the Grande Island beach, were transformed into barracks.

The influx changed life for those at Subic, too. Lines lengthened at the post exchange and commissaries. The arrival of Clark's personnel also brought 4,000 additional cars to the normally quiet streets of the base.

"It was a very difficult situation because in less than 24 hours, Subic Bay became a whole little city," said Maj. Wayne Crist, normally assigned to the Clark public affairs office.

JUNE 21, 1991

▶ Volcano blows, 1A

The Story—Part 3

DISCOVERY FILE

The Rock Cycle

If you were to hike up Mount Rainier, you'd see many kinds of rocks—black, gray, crumbly, bumpy, and so on. But all the different types of rock can be classified as igneous, sedimentary, or metamorphic. *Igneous* rocks come either from volcanoes at the surface or from magma that didn't quite reach the surface. *Sedimentary* rock forms when tiny mineral grains, which eroded from other rocks, settle somewhere, such as at a river bottom, and combine to form new rock. Rock that begins as igneous or sedimentary rock and then is changed by heat and pressure is called *metamorphic* rock.

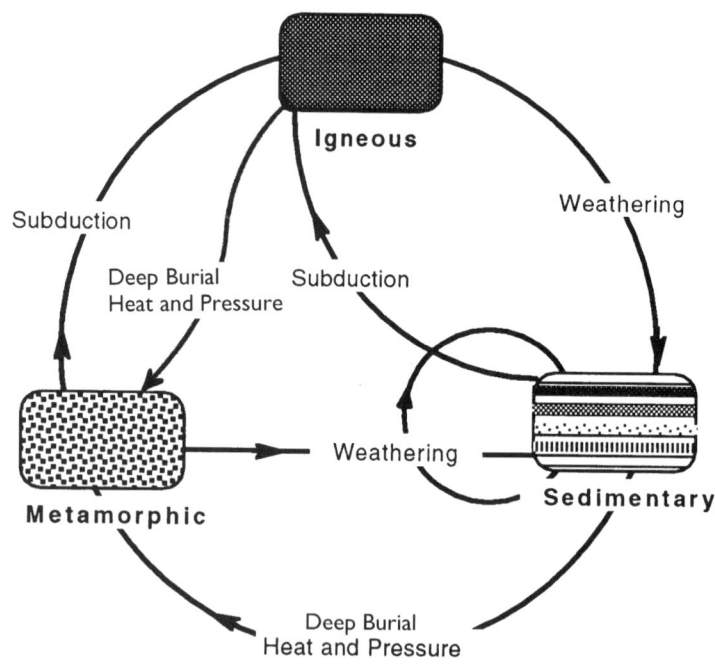

Forces that Change Rocks

Right below your feet, our planet is alive with forces inside and out. These forces drive the rock cycle—an ongoing process that builds, destroys, and rebuilds the rocks that form the crust of our Earth. As you might imagine, this is a very time-consuming process.

Internal forces are created by currents of molten rock that rise and spread out in the mantle (the layer below the crust). These are thought to be the forces that move the tectonic plates.

On Earth's surface, the main external force is something you experience every day: the weather. Weathering and erosion—by rain, wind, snow, and glaciers—wear down exposed rocks of all kinds. Rivers carry the rock debris to lakes and oceans where it collects as sediment. Some sediments stick together and become sedimentary rock.

When Earth's tectonic plates collide, they may push sedimentary rock above the sea to form islands, mountains, and other land forms. (This sedimentary rock, now exposed to the forces of weathering, can be worn down by erosion to become a new generation of sedimentary rock.) Plates undergoing subduction—where one plate plunges under another—carry igneous and sedimentary rocks down into the mantle, where heat and pressure transform them into metamorphic rock.

Molten igneous rock rises through the cooler, denser rocks surrounding volcanoes. The volcanic activity creates island arcs, such as Alaska's Aleutian Islands. It also puts new material into the continental crust and bakes pre-existing rocks.

Igneous Rocks

Igneous rocks contain many minerals, primarily *silicates*. Silicates are compounds formed from silica (a combination of silicon and oxygen) and any of various metal oxides. Silica is found in quartz and opal. Silicon is the second most abundant element on Earth after oxygen.

The major silicate minerals are called *feldspars*. Granite, which is made up of quartz, feldspar, and mica, is the chief igneous rock of the continental crust.

The type of igneous rock that forms depends on what the magma is made of and what happens to it as it cools. Different minerals crystallize or "freeze out" and separate at different temperatures. The rate of cooling determines the size of these crystals. Slow cooling produces rocks with large crystals; fast cooling generates fine-grained rocks.

DISCOVERY FILE

Volcano Monitoring and Prediction

Prediction is the science behind the guesswork. Given the unpredictability of a volcano, what are the best ways to monitor changes—visible as well as hidden—that signal the makings of an eruption?

Volcano observatories are located at a number of sites around the globe. From such locations as the observatories in Hawaii, Washington, and Alaska, systematic and continuous monitoring of a volcano and its surroundings takes place. What volcanologists do at these sites is observe what happens and keep a detailed diary of changes and events.

What can scientists monitor? Between eruptions, they can mark increases or decreases in the amount of steam coming from vents; see whether new steam areas or ground cracks develop; study the widening of old cracks; note withering plant life; or watch for changing color in mineral deposits around fumaroles.

A more dramatic signal is an actual change in the shape of a volcano. The volcano gradually swells or inflates as magma rises into its "plumbing system."

After an eruption begins, there are additional monitoring tasks. On paper and on film, scientists document the course of the eruption. They make temperature measurements of lava and gas. They measure ash plumes. They collect eruptive products for later analysis. They gauge and record the height of

Geologists collect gas samples.

Geologists use a theodolite to measure angles and slope-distance to the lava dome.

IN THE NEWS

```
From:  IN%"rmuffley@vita.org
To:    IN%"ldavid@delphi.com
CC:
Subj:  Rains, Mud, and Pinatubo
Date:  Fri, 23 Sep 1994 11:16:01 -0400 (EDT)
PHILIPPINES - LAHAR
DHA-GENEVA INFORMATION REPORT NO.1
23 SEPTEMBER 1994
```

1. HEAVY RAINS ON 22 SEPTEMBER 1994 IN THE REGION OF MOUNT PINATUBO VOLCANO TRIGGERED MUDFLOWS CONSISTING OF TONNES OF ASH AND OTHER DEBRIS, KNOWN AS LAHAR, EJECTED ON THE SLOPES OF PINATUBO BY THE VOLCANIC ERUPTION OF 1991.

2. THE PHILIPPINE INSTITUTE OF VOLCANOLOGY AND SIESMOLOGY (PHIVOLCS) REPORTS THAT UP TO TEN FEET HIGH LAHAR FLOWED DOWN THE PASIG-POTRERO RIVER IN PAMPANGA CAUSING THE BREACHING OF MANY DIKES.

3. THE NATIONAL DISASTER COORDINATING COUNCIL INDICATES THAT 500 HOUSES AND ONE DEPT. OF PUBLIC WORKS AND HIGHWAYS (DPWH) WERE TOTALLY BURIED. PRELIMINARY REPORTS SHOW FIVE DEAD AND SEVEN MISSING.

4. GOVERNMENT TEAMS EFFECTING RESCUE AND EVACUATION OPERATIONS IN THE AFFECTED AREA. 29 HOMELESS FAMILIES WERE ACCOMMODATED IN PUBLIC BUILDINGS.

5. THE GOVERNMENT HAS NOT REQUESTED INTERNATIONAL ASSISTANCE. UNDP/DHA RESIDENT REPRESENTATIVE FOLLOWING SITUATION IN CLOSE COOPERATION WITH CENTRAL AUTHORITIES.

+DEPARTMENT OF HUMANITARIAN AFFAIRS=

Actual e-mail report of continuing Pinatubo devastation

lava fountains and the rates of lava flows.

Volcano monitoring also involves ground movements. Even the smallest earthquakes are noted—some too faint to be felt. Changes in local electrical and magnetic fields are important. These changes may signify pressure changes and other stresses caused by the movement of magma below ground.

What's in a volcanologist's tool kit? Among the items are electronic tiltmeters and laser-beam instruments called *Geodimeters*™. These are used to measure changes in the slope or tilt of a volcano by shining a laser beam to a reflector on the volcano. The round-trip travel time of that signal can give a very accurate measurement of volcanic movement.

A network of seismic instruments is typically placed around a volcano. Earthquakes can provide the earliest warning of volcanic unrest. Data gathered by seismometers are sent by radio or satellite to a central location for computer analysis. Volcanologists also use automated video time-lapse cameras to record volcanic outbursts. They use devices that monitor changes in the composition of gases coming out of a volcano. Emission rates of sulfur dioxide escaping from a fumarole, for example, can be measured by this equipment.

In easily accessible areas, scientists wearing asbestos gloves and gas masks to protect themselves often collect samples of volcanic gases from active vents.

Although these instruments are helpful in monitoring volcanic activity, predicting the exact time of an eruption is still very hard. However, keeping a scientific eye on the behavior of volcanoes is critical for both land-use planning and, above all, public safety.

Improving our knowledge about volcanic phenomena provides clues about Earth's past and present—as well as its future.

ON THE JOB

Volcanologist

DR. RICHARD FISKE
SMITHSONIAN INSTITUTION
MUSEUM OF NATURAL HISTORY
WASHINGTON, DC

What appealed to me as a child was the "romance" of being a geologist in a distant land and living out of tents on expeditions. That's how it really was then; it was great! Looking at *National Geographic* magazines and seeing pictures of exciting activities in far-off places—that was very stimulating. I also had the role model of an uncle who was an oil-company geologist in South America. At that time, it was frontier down there. It was exciting work. So I wanted to be a geologist.

At Princeton University I majored in geological engineering, and I loved it. I pursued a career as an oil company geologist in graduate school, but there I was influenced by two professors. They had a small research grant to support the two of them and a graduate student to work at Mount Rainier.

We worked on a contract with the National Park Service to prepare a geologic map of Mount Rainier National Park. The mountains there are tall. Mount Rainier itself is huge, like a big ice cream cone sitting in the middle of the park. It was hard work. I wasn't exposed to backpacking when I was growing up, although I do it now very often.

My fieldwork now is divided between two places—Hawaii and Japan. In Hawaii I collaborate with U.S. Geological Survey colleagues. We're mapping cracks and structures in the Kilauea volcano. The whole volcano is in the process of moving apart. It's unbelievable. Half the volcano is separating from the other half and moving into the ocean. A huge piece of the island that's three miles thick is moving about 10 centimeters a year at the surface, and that's really fast. Near the base of the volcano at a depth of nine kilometers, it's estimated to be moving 25 centimeters a year. That makes it the fastest-moving fault in the world.

One of these huge landslides happened on the west side of the Mauna Loa volcano more than 100,000 years ago. It was a big event that caused a *tsunami*, a sea wave, that ran 282 meters (925 feet) up the side of another Hawaiian island, Lanai. That's almost twice as high as the Washington Monument.

Eventually another piece of the big island of Hawaii will fall off, but it probably won't happen within our lifetime.

The sea floor around the Hawaiian Islands shows that sections of older volcanoes of the Hawaiian Islands chain have collapsed and fallen into the ocean. This process is constantly going on. Individual pieces—the size of Manhattan Island in New York City—have slid down 200 kilometers across the sea floor. It's a hot topic! It's going to change our whole way of thinking about volcanology of big-island volcanoes like those in Hawaii.

When volcanoes break apart and collapse, it's called *volcano spreading*. Volcanoes have "underground plumbing systems" where magma comes up from the mantle and spreads out inside the volcano. It's now realized that this magma is pushing apart the volcano, like a bulldozer, and it pushes the entire side of the volcano off. The physical scale of this phenomenon is something we've never seen before because we never had the means to measure it.

One of the most important technological breakthroughs is the Global Positioning System (GPS) of satellites. We can come back to the same location again and again and determine whether that area is moving. We had other means of measuring before, but they were not very precise. GPS is really precise.

➤ continued on page 42

▶ continued from page 41

The other half of my field work is in Japan, which in some ways is even more technology driven. My Japanese colleagues and I are gaining access to the Japanese research submarines. We are going into underwater volcanoes south of Japan that are extraordinary. Unlike midocean ridge-type volcanoes where "pillow" lava comes out slowly, these are the result of big caldera eruptions like the one that created Crater Lake in Oregon. Imagine the whole Crater Lake structure 800 meters (about half a mile) under water.

Submarine volcanoes of this type have huge mineral deposits. The reason is this: in eruptions on land, a lot of the metals come to the surface in gases and literally blow away. You can smell sulfur gases and other metals. Some metals are taken away in the stream water, but they tend not to be concentrated so much.

In the ocean, these substances hit the cold sea water and precipitate, so the volcano is jetting mineral deposits. Over the last 20 years, geologists have discovered that many of the important mines in the United States, Canada, Japan, South Africa, and other places were ancient submarine volcanoes that became exposed on land.

What is it like to climb into a submersible and visit an underwater volcano? It is unbelievable! The first submersible I went down in was the *Alvin*, the small U.S. research submarine.

We were inside a chamber about six feet, two inches in diameter. We went down 1,400 meters (more than 4,000 feet). That's not deep by marine-science standards, but in volcanology that's deep enough. We were down for about seven hours and spent about five hours on the bottom. We cruised around looking at the terrain and taking samples.

Part of the eruption deposit is a layer of pumice stone about 90 meters (300 feet) thick. It looks and is loose like popcorn. The submersible's manipulator arm could pick up just two or three of these nuggets and put them in a basket. So when I came back to the United States, I went to a farm-supply store and bought a metal feed scoop, like the kind you feed horses with. We attached that scoop so the manipulator arm could grab more pumice. Now we can scoop up 500 pieces of pumice at a time!

If you are interested in a career in earth sciences, the advice universally given is to take math, physics, and chemistry in high school and college and to do well in them. Those core courses are very important.

On Mount Rainier
If I were working with your team to plan a television program on Mount Rainier, first I would study a topographical map of the area. Remember that the greatest hazards at Rainier are mudflows and avalanches that tend to travel down the valley floors. Look about 60 to 80 kilometers (about 40 to 50 miles) down the mountain top to see what towns are in the valleys. What is the population in the valley bottoms?

Lava is not the worst danger. Floods of debris and water are. All Pacific Northwest volcanoes that are classified as active will erupt eventually, but what distinguishes Mount Rainier as a threat is the huge amount of water in the form of ice and snow. About 4.4 cubic kilometers (2.7 cubic miles) of water are tied up in solid form on Mount Rainier. If the volcano heats up, melted ice and snow could produce mudflows. They would flow down valleys into populated areas.

The Pacific Northwest is also the site of large earthquakes that are related not to volcanoes but to movement along faults in the area. Strong ground motion associated with earthquakes can cause volcanoes to partly collapse, producing huge avalanches.

One difference between volcanoes and other mountains such as Pikes Peak is that those mountains are there because of uplift and erosion. Erosion takes away the softest material and leaves the hardest rock on the mountain. Volcanoes are exactly the opposite. They are the products of eruptions of material onto the surface. Eruptions build huge mountains that are very crumbly and soft. Volcanoes are very susceptible to failure, either because water gets involved and makes mudflows or because earthquakes shake the volcano apart.

What is the best way to evacuate people if the volcano becomes dangerous? It certainly isn't to escape down the roads that follow the valleys. The best place to go is up about 60 meters (200 feet) above the valley floor.

If you travel to the area below Mount Rainier, you'll see new developments being built on the flat valley floors. Why are these valleys flat? They are the surfaces of a big mudflow deposit from Mount Rainier laid down a few centuries ago. Because the period between eruptions is long, people forget the potential danger. There are also economic pressures to use the land. The flat valley floors are easy to build on and are fertile for growing. It's difficult for government to keep people away from such desirable land, but they're trying. Changes in zoning can make it more expensive to live in hazardous areas. When an area is zoned hazardous, its insurance rates and loan rates go up.

That's how geologists get involved. They assess the risk that helps determine the zoning. In Hawaii, there is a map of the Kilauea lava-flow area designating high-risk zones. Great care is taken in producing hazard maps that are scientifically defensible. Areas at high risk for earthquakes are zoned this way, too.

As world population increases, there will be an even greater need for people to live close to hazardous areas, especially volcanoes. This means there is more of a need for understanding volcanoes and how they will threaten people in the area.

Our understanding of earth-science processes is going to change. Earth sciences involve lots of factors that we don't thoroughly understand. As you learn more, you realize it's more complex. What we are trying to do at Mount Rainier is carry out the work before a possible crisis. We need to understand the processes ourselves and then transmit this knowledge to citizens, city officials, fire departments, and police forces. Then they can educate others and make evacuation plans.

DISCOVERY FILE

The Attraction of Mount Vesuvius

Mount Vesuvius has a history of eruptions dating back thousands of years. This destroyer has been in a state of frequent eruptive activity for the past 300 years.

Vesuvius unleashed its force in 79 A.D., burying the Roman towns of Pompeii and Herculaneum so thoroughly that they were "lost" for hundreds of years. It was not until 1738 that Pompeii and Herculaneum were exposed to light again. Scientists discovered an outdoor theater in Herculaneum. It was the first clue that the ancient city destroyed by Vesuvius had been found. Among other artifacts, a bronze horse head was found at the theater site.

Mount Vesuvius is located eight miles from the large city of Naples. It has driven people from their homes time and time again, only to have following generations reclaim the site. There is an irresistible lure to rebuild and replant on the risky slopes of the volcano. Laden with volcanic ash, the soil is so rich that three full crops, instead of one, can be harvested each year.

Vesuvius draws not only the wonder of neighboring villagers but also volcanologists anxious to gather the latest scientific data about the volcano. To be able to correctly predict its next eruption is the ultimate prize.

Vesuvius' last moderately sized eruption took place in 1631. The volcano has been fairly quiet since 1944. Between 1631 and 1944, Vesuvius had no period of inactivity longer than seven years.

Scientists chart eruptions looking for patterns. A pattern in the data seems to divide Vesuvian activity into eight cycles of 2,000 years each, covering a 17,000-year span. Every 2,000-year cycle begins with an explosive eruption of Vesuvius.

Eruption precursors have also been noted. For example, the crater floor lowered before the 1906 eruption. A similar drop took place in 1964, and between 1970 and 1974, the floor sank another five feet. Also, an earthquake preceded the destruction of Pompeii and Herculaneum. Perhaps an earthquake, or series of earthquakes, in the area should be a signal for Vesuvius watchers.

A study completed in 1994 found that a large or even moderate eruption of Mount Vesuvius could affect an area where between 200,000 and 1,000,000 people live. The study recommended new roads and plans for evacuating people rapidly.

The Story—Part 4
Global Impact

The violent eruptions of Mount Pinatubo sent huge amounts of gas high into the earth's stratosphere. In a single episode, Pinatubo threw nearly as much sulfur dioxide into the upper atmosphere as is emitted by U.S. factories in a whole year.

Picked up by the earth's global wind system, the veil of sulfuric acid particles made from the sulfur dioxide drifted around the equator from east to west.

Satellite sensors monitored the cloud. These orbiting instruments indicated that within days after the major eruption, the cloud formed a nearly continuous band that stretched roughly 7,000 miles from Indonesia to central Africa. One spacecraft found that more than 19 million tons of sulfur dioxide were carried more than 18 miles high into the atmosphere.

These quantities of particles in the atmosphere absorbed and reflected solar radiation and affected the earth's protective ozone layer.

Tiny sulfuric acid droplets—also called *aerosols*—blocked out some of the sun's warming rays, sending them back out into space and thereby cooling the earth. This effect lasted through early 1994. The temporary cooling equaled a decrease in global surface temperatures of approximately 1 degree Fahrenheit. The cooling caused by Mount Pinatubo was estimated to be 60 percent greater than any other climate disturbance since 1976.

Mount Pinatubo's climatic influence also seems to have made it easier for human-made chlorofluo-

STUDENT VOICES

We left Clark Air Base and drove to Subic Bay Naval Base. The drive took a long time, because so many people were evacuating. We had to live with a Navy family for a few days until we were evacuated from the Philippines. While we stayed in their house, we had no electricity or water. Ashes were on the ground as deep as snow, making it very hard to drive.

The eruption came during a typhoon. There was rain, ashes, wind, and earthquakes. At noon, it was dark as midnight. There was thunder and lightening and the sound of pouring rain mixed with hail, but it wasn't hail, it was volcanic ash.

The ashes and rain were so heavy that they tore down buildings. When we were at Subic Bay Naval Base, a building collapsed and two girls died.

Be sure your television show tells how scientists can predict when a volcano may erupt. Their predictions saved our lives.

Michelle Strother
Yorktown, VA

rocarbons (CFCs) to destroy the ozone layer. How? The chlorine compounds that destroy the ozone are released when CFCs reach the stratosphere and begin to break up. Scientists believe that, with the addition of the sulfuric acid particles from the Pinatubo eruption, the ozone-destroying chlorine compounds may have been converted into more active forms of chlorine, which can cause a dramatic increase in ozone depletion. Reductions in ozone permit more ultraviolet radiation to strike the earth. An increase in ultraviolet radiation has been linked to increased skin cancers, cataracts, and even the withering of crops. The total climatic effects that can be directly linked to Pinatubo are expected to take many years to sort out.

Mount Pinatubo's reawakening in 1991 was a powerful reminder that we live on a truly active planet. The staggering consequences of volcanic eruptions involve not only geologic change, but people, property, and climate—all on a planetary scale.

Volcanic events show that the world is a living laboratory. The eruption of Mount Pinatubo yielded important information to help predict volcanic hazards in the future and to help us coexist today with the constructive and destructive forces of nature. ■

IN THE NEWS

Volcano eases but U.S. flying families home

By Juan J. Walte
USA TODAY

Fears of a catastrophic eruption by Mount Pinatubo have eased today, but the threat to life and property still concerns Philippine and U.S. officials.

The eruptions, including Saturday's massive blast, have buried parts of the Philippines under tons of volcanic ash.

U.S. officials today are beginning to evacuate 20,000 military dependents to the United States. They had been at Clark Air Base, 8½ miles from Pinatubo, and Subic Bay and Cubi Point naval facilities.

Navy officials said the daughter of a U.S. enlisted man died when a roof collapsed late Saturday at Subic.

The Red Cross said at least 76 people have died — most as buildings collapsed from the weight of ash — since the volcano, dormant for 611 years, stirred again June 9.

Thousands of Filipinos have fled the stricken area. Cars, buses and trucks, caked with ash, inched south along jammed roads toward Manila.

Experts had feared a cataclysmic explosion in which Pinatubo could blow itself apart. But now:

▶ Pinatubo's "top has been blown and replaced by a large crater . . . about one mile across," Robert Wesson, U.S. Geological Survey, said Sunday. "Mount Pinatubo as it existed Friday no longer exists."

▶ "The likelihood of a violent eruption is now considerably reduced," Jerry Diolata of the Philippine Institute of Volcanology and Seismology said early today. But an "avalanche now seems likely to happen."

Heavy rains in a weekend tropical storm soaked the ash and triggered mud flows.

Raymundo Punongbayan, director of the Philippine vulcanology institute, said he might recommend reducing the 25-mile danger zone around the volcano but would wait until an aerial inspection, possibly today.

A spreading cloud of smoke hangs over the islands, impeding air traffic.

"You couldn't see your hand in front of your face," said Lt. Cmdr. Kevin Mukri, Subic Bay spokesman. It's "like going through the worst snowstorm you've ever experienced."

The ash was carried by winds as far west as Cambodia.

Meanwhile, in Japan, a lava-filled dome in the crater of Mount Unzen rose 65 feet Sunday, prompting authorities to warn of another eruption. One earlier this month killed 39.

JUNE 17, 1991

ON THE JOB

Two Special-Effects Experts

DAVID CARSON
INDUSTRIAL LIGHT AND MAGIC
MARIN COUNTY, CA

I am a visual-effects supervisor. That means I'm responsible for delivering all the visual effects in a movie to the film director's specifications.

One of the films I worked on was *Joe Versus the Volcano*, starring Tom Hanks and Meg Ryan. It was my job to supervise the creation of all the film that had the volcano special effects.

I've been interested in special effects for a long time. As a young boy, I watched movies with special effects and wondered, "How did they do that?" I read articles about the people who worked on special effects and how "movie magic" was done. That inspired me, and through perseverance and luck, I was able to enter the movie business.

I have been in this field for 18 years and enjoy it very much. I started working for Industrial Light and Magic 15 years ago—just about halfway through the making of the movie *The Empire Strikes Back*. Over the years, I've worked with both George Lucas and Steven Spielberg on their special-effects needs.

On *Joe Versus the Volcano*, we started putting our special-effects plans together by doing research. We spent time in research libraries looking at documentary footage and photographs of real volcanoes, such as those in Hawaii. We also studied how the movie *Krakatoa, East of Java* and other films created their volcano scenes.

Early films, for the most part, built models of volcanoes and made them as large as possible. Then movie makers began to use pyrotechnics—fireworks and explosive charges—to create the effect of a volcanic eruption. Because pyrotechnics happen faster than an eruption, we film with high-speed cameras and then later slow down the film to give the impression of a real erupting volcano.

For *Joe Versus the Volcano*, the director wanted more of a fantasy look to the volcano, rather than a totally realistic one. So we took a layered, artificial approach. We used lots of lights, steam, and background paintings behind the model. You could use a similar approach in creating your own volcano special effects.

Our volcano model was sculptured mostly out of plaster and then painted to give it a more realistic look. It was used for the distant camera shots. It's best to build as large a model as you reasonably can. We also placed tubes in the plaster, which vented either dry-ice vapor, steam, or smoke from under the model.

For close-ups looking down into the volcano from the rim, we used a plastic tray 2.5 meters (about 8 feet) in diameter. You could use one a foot or two across. We randomly placed strips of red and yellow cellophane on the bottom. The strips produced orange in places where they crossed each other. The lava was a mixture of gooey liquid in the tray. You could try corn syrup. We sprinkled some crushed-up charcoal on top. Underneath the tray, red lights gave you the feeling that red hot lava was deep inside the volcano. All this combined to create the innards of a volcano!

Although this approach worked for our fantasy volcano, most films requiring special effects now use computers. Over the last few years, computers have had a profound impact on the movie-making industry.

A typical day for me starts in the screening room where we spend 30 to 45 minutes reviewing everything filmed the day before. We look at scenes and decide whether the film is ready to be sent to the director. If it's not ready, we discuss what we like, what needs more work, and how to do things differently. All this involves the camera people, model builders, and other technicians. I also spend time in the cutting room where we edit film.

If you're interested in a career in special effects, it's important to take a lot of art classes and to be able to communicate by sketches. I also recommend taking courses that give you a sense of what makes for a good film versus a bad film. Take film-history and film-appreciation classes.

I have some suggestions for creating a television program on Mount Rainier. Make sure your visuals explain the basic principles behind volcanoes, whether you use film clips, graphics, charts, or simple drawings. These are key tools in making documentary films.

Also, when you're shooting, use a tripod whenever possible to get a steady image. You can cut in and out of footage of an interview by showing some attractive visuals to reinforce points made by the person being interviewed. That makes it easier for your audience to understand and grasp the points in your film.

You don't have to use only still shots. Start out with a close shot on one area of a photo or painting, and then move the camera slowly across the scene to another area. You can also start out close and gradually pull the camera lens back to show the whole visual, or you can do the reverse.

We use math and science every day in our work. One of the ways we make fantastic things seem believable is to imitate the laws of physics. We look at how things work in the real world. We study how gravity affects something falling, or how an object accelerates, or even the way water acts when you punch into it and how water droplets form. We use math to figure out the scale of how far away from a model we need to be filming so the model looks realistic, and we use math when we're shooting at different speeds to simulate reality.

Our computer programmers' work is very math intensive. You have to understand how the real world works in order to create believable movies. Physics, chemistry, and math come up in a number of surprising ways in my work. It didn't seem like that would have been the case when I was a kid watching monsters rampage around on the screen!

LORNE PETERSON
INDUSTRIAL LIGHT AND MAGIC
MARIN COUNTY, CA

I'm a model maker for Industrial Light and Magic. I was a member of the team that created the lava scenes in the movie *Congo*. I've also made models for movies like the *Indiana Jones* series, the *Star Wars* series, *China Syndrome*, and many others.

In planning the lava scenes for *Congo*, we researched volcanoes in other films. We also studied films of actual volcanoes. As we looked through some of the older footage, we were disappointed. A lot of the lava looked like oatmeal mixed with red paint.

We wanted a "real" look for our lava. We played around with all kinds of materials: we used melted dark chocolate with hunks of white chocolate floating on top, and we tried flour-and-water mixtures. There are many, many ways to do anything. Even if all you have is broken-up pieces of cork and tomato ketchup or marshmallow sauce, somehow you'll make it work.

We finally decided to use a product called Methacel. Methacel is a powdered food additive used to thicken ketchup, jams, jellies, and other foods. It's an edible, inexpensive fiber with no nutritional value. Methacel is short for methylcellulose. Methacel is made from ground-up wood fiber.

We mixed the Methacel with warm water using a paint mixer. You add more water to make it thinner and more powder to make it thicker. The result is a slimy-looking substance.

Methacel is whitish, but we wanted our lava to have a black crust with streaks of gray. For color, we tried adding food coloring. We also tried paint pigments. We eventually decided to have our computer-graphics department colorize it. To put a crust on your lava, you can dust the top with black powdered tempera.

To look real, the crust must travel with the molten lava beneath it. When you build your model, be sure that the area where the lava is waiting to flow—the holding tank—is the same width as the trough you are letting the lava flow down. If the holding tank is wider, the crust won't act like real lava. It'll get ripped off. So if you want a lava flow five centimeters wide, your holding tank also needs to be five centimeters wide and two or three centimeters deep.

▶ continued on page 48

continued from page 47

You can put curves in your trough. Your lava will react like the crust really would. Some of it will hang up on the side of the bank, and some will be thinner on the far side.

The tank that holds the pre-flow lava will probably need to go back about two or three meters, depending on how many seconds you want the lava to flow. The trough can be hinged so that when you're ready for lights, camera, and action, you just sprinkle the crust on top and tilt the holding tank up, and the lava will flow into the trough.

In *Congo*, there are also some long-distance shots of the volcano blowing up. When you attempt to simulate that, you have to understand what's really happening during an eruption. The magma starts to rise inside the volcano. As it rises, it lifts the ground. This could be a few inches or several feet.

The groundwater in the different layers of the mountain begins to find new channels as the ground lifts and cracks. The groundwater rushes downward into deeper levels. It stops when it hits hot magma. It instantly turns to steam and tries to expand. That's what causes the giant explosion in some volcanoes. With Mount St. Helens, there was a lot of water, so a big explosion blew a quarter of the mountain off the top.

To simulate this, we used a balloon underneath fine dirt. We took a one-foot diameter balloon and covered it. From the bottom, we raised the balloon slightly, which made the earth appear to crack open. Then we stuck the balloon with a pin. The balloon popped, and the "land" collapsed. I understand that your Science Activity called "Pop Goes the Volcano" is very similar to this.

The footage in *Congo* that shows lava flowing down the volcano from a distance is of a real volcano in Costa Rica. Our film crew shot footage of the volcano when it was steaming a little. Then our computer-graphics people added smoke and lava flow with their computers.

IN THE NEWS

Evacuees: 'Ready to go home'

By Deeann Glamser
USA TODAY

McCHORD AIR FORCE BASE, Wash. — Forgive Mark and Tina Brown if they're a little negative about tropical life.

"We had an earthquake, a typhoon and a volcano all at once," said Mark Brown, 23 years old and very tired. "I'm ready to go home."

Brown and his wife will visit relatives in Mississippi — and then they're moving to Alaska.

Their story is one of the first out of Mount Pinatubo's eruption: They're among an estimated 20,000 evacuees heading here from two U.S. bases in the Philippines.

Many left with a few suitcases and no hopes of salvaging anything else. They've seen their homes destroyed under volcanic ash. They've had little food, no running water or electricity. They've spent as long as two days crowded on naval ships and 18 hours on planes.

"We've been packed like sardines for 10 days," said Susan Breier. "I want to get away from all these people."

The Breiers were evacuated from Clark Air Base and then returned — arriving back at their home minutes before the volcano blew.

"It was absolute silence," said Cliff Breier, an Air Force captain. "You couldn't hear a bird, nothing. This huge cloud of gray ash just floated up."

They grabbed a few things and jumped into a police van.

Cathy Lara, 29, six months pregnant, cried: "It was raining sand. There was thunder and lightning, and the earth was rumbling."

John Ector, 18, said he'll never forget his high school graduation speech to 53 classmates at Subic Bay. "My last line was, 'Life is an adventure to be savored.'" Two days later, ash collapsed the theater where the ceremony was held.

McChord is the main processing point for evacuees. Flights, expected for 10 days, began arriving late Tuesday.

The Red Cross is handing out sweatshirts, and the Salvation Army brought in racks of used clothing for people who abandoned most of their own.

"Whatever was left behind, they can assume they'll never see again," said Air Force Capt. John Litten. Clark is buried under 2 feet of ash and rocks.

People waiting here for flights home swap volcano stories, praise rescue missions and snack on cookies and juice.

Evacuees are issued emergency cash or advance pay, and receive military-paid airline tickets to anywhere in the USA. Family pets get special quick-clearance. AT&T and US West Inc. set up free phone banks so evacuees can talk to families.

Francisco Sanding, 59, spent two days at the base trying to find his sailor nephew, boiler chief Gregory Giron. Said Sanding, "I'm just taking a chance, hoping that he'll come this way."

JUNE 20, 1991

SCIENCE ACTIVITY

Do You Tire of Fire?

Purpose
To investigate volcano formation, structure, and location.

Background
Mount Rainier has recently been selected as a "decade volcano." This means Mount Rainier will be carefully monitored and studied by scientists during the next 10 years.

Being selected a "decade volcano" has dramatically increased the number of visitors to the region. Officials at Mount Rainier National Park have been very busy and need to update their old volcano display. They've heard about your television program and are anxious to view the final product. The park superintendent wants to use the program as part of a permanent volcano display. Your project coordinator would like your company to produce other materials that can be included with the volcano display. The display needs to have the following components:

1. Explain how volcanoes form near spreading plates, hot spots, and subduction zones. Remember to emphasize volcanoes in the Cascade Range.
2. Compare the types of eruptions that produce cinder-cone, shield, and composite volcanoes.
3. Provide two world maps showing the relationship between volcanoes and earthquakes. (Use volcano and earthquake coordinates to prepare the maps.) The maps should also show the different types of plate boundaries found in areas of intense tectonic (earthquake and volcanic) activity.

Materials
For each team of five students
- Reference materials relating to plate tectonics
- Cardboard, poster board, and construction paper
- Box
- Scissors
- Tape and glue
- Two copies of a world map (from teacher)
- Two different-colored pencils
- Earthquakes and Volcano Coordinates sheet (page 50)

Procedure
1. Complete your background research on volcanoes. Divide the team into two groups, and split up the different parts of the display.

➤ continued on page 50

Μεμο To: Εαρτηλινγσ

Φρομ: Πλανετ οφ Ζορτ, Ηιγη Χουνσελ

Συβφεχτ: Τασκ Περφορμανχε

Ωε ωουλδ αππρεχιατε ψουρ χοοπερατιον ιν αδδρεσσινγ τηε φολλοωινγ τοπιχσ:

1. Εξπλαιν το υσ ωηατ α πλατε ισ.

2. Ηοω δο πλατεσ μοϖε?

3. Ωηψ δο ϖολχανοεσ σεεμ το βε χλοσε το πλατε εδγεσ?

4. Χαν ϖολχανοεσ βε ιν τηε μιδδλε οφ α πλατε? Ωηερε δοεσ τηισ ηαππεν ον ψουρ πλανετ?

5. Ωηατ κινδ οφ λαϖα χαν ωε εξπεχτ φρομ συβδυχτιον ζονε ερυπτιονσ?

6. Ωηερε δο ψου ηαϖε συβδυχτιον ζονεσ ιν ψουρ ωορλδ?

The Story—Part 4

▶ continued from page 49

2. Create the display with the components listed in Background.
3. Make a three-dimensional representation of a volcano. Be sure to show at least part of the volcano in cross section. Show external and internal igneous features common to volcanoes and volcanic regions. Use your imagination to come up with ways to entertain and educate park visitors.

Conclusion

1. Describe differences and similarities among the three types of volcanoes.
2. The diagram below shows a cross section of a part of the planet Zort. There has been no volcanic activity on this planet for millions of years. Now, however, the Zortarians are reporting that there are increasing numbers of earthquakes around smoking areas of their planet. (The nonsmoking areas remain calm.) Zortarians think there will be volcanic eruptions in a very short time. Since you are from Earth, where there are many volcanoes, Zortarian officials have asked you to locate on their map all locations where volcanoes might pop up. In addition, they want you to predict the type of volcano they might expect at each site.
3. The Zortarians have sent you a memo. Translate the memo and answer the questions for the Zortarians.

Volcano Event Locations		
Volcanic Event	Degrees Longitude	Degrees Latitude
1	150 W	60 N
2	70 W	35 S
3	120 W	45 N
4	61 W	15 N
5	105 W	20 N
6	75 W	0
7	122 W	40 N
8	30 E	40 N
9	44 E	15 N
10	160 E	55 N
11	37 E	3 S
12	145 E	40 N
13	120 E	10 S
14	14 E	41 N
15	105 E	5 S
16	35 E	15 N
17	70 W	30 S
18	15 W	65 N
19	25 W	17 N
20	155 E	5 S
21	60 E	15 S
22	25 W	55 S
23	27 W	38 N
24	13 W	37 S
25	71 W	16 S
26	170 E	23 S
27	164 E	10 S
28	178 W	52 N
29	38 E	03 N
30	90 W	17 N

Earthquake Event Locations		
Quake Event	Degrees Longitude	Degrees Latitude
1	170 W	50 N
2	160 W	55 N
3	154 W	60 N
4	118 W	33 N
5	5 W	18 N
6	80 W	10 S
7	70 W	30 S
8	157 W	20 N
9	80 W	33 N
10	44 W	10 N
11	45 W	20 N
12	30 W	40 N
13	20 W	65 N
14	20 W	0
15	125 E	10 N
16	125 E	22 N
17	110 E	10 S
18	123 E	0
19	135 E	35 N
20	142 E	38 N
21	160 E	54 N
22	150 E	45 N
23	124 W	62 N
24	151 E	10 S
25	179 W	35 S
26	153 E	04 S
27	128 W	44 N
28	25 W	60 S
29	28 W	01 N
30	114 W	44 N

Volcano!

Discovery File

Volcanoes and Global Climate Change

Volcanoes are thought to be responsible for the global cooling that scientists observe during the years after a major eruption. The amount and extent of cooling seem to depend on the time of the year, the force of the eruption and its latitude. When large amounts of material from an erupting volcano reach the stratosphere, they can produce a widespread cooling effect. The global cooling that followed the eruption of Mount Pinatubo is an example of this.

As volcanoes erupt, they blast huge clouds into the atmosphere. These clouds are made up of particles and gases. The gas that concerns us most when it comes to cooling is sulfur dioxide (SO_2). Millions of tons of sulfur dioxide gas can reach the stratosphere from a major volcano. The sulfur dioxide reacts with water vapor to become particles of sulfuric acid.

$$2(SO_2) + 2(H_2O) \longrightarrow 2H_2SO_4$$

These particles reflect some of the sun's energy and prevent the normal solar heating of Earth's atmosphere.

Past periods of global cooling have been linked with major historic eruptions. The year 1816 was called "the year without a summer." It was a time of weather-related disruptions in New England and western Europe. Killing frosts were reported during the summer of 1816 in the United States and Canada. These strange phenomena were linked to the eruption of the Tambora volcano in Indonesia the year before. Sulfuric acid particles from Tambora not only changed the weather thousands of miles away, but they also led to brilliant sunsets seen around the world for several years.

NASA

Not all of the evidence supports the link between eruptions and cooling. Two recent events have provided contradictory evidence. In 1963, Mount Agung on the Indonesian island of Bali apparently caused a considerable decrease in temperatures around much of the world, but when Mexico's El Chichón erupted in 1982, there was little effect. There are many other factors that influence Earth's climate. Perhaps the locations of these two volcanoes were different enough to account for the difference in impact. Perhaps the El Niño that occurred in 1982 was a factor. El Niño is a Pacific Ocean phenomenon that causes worldwide weather changes. These changes may have canceled out the effects, if any, of the El Chichón eruption.

The evidence leads to many questions. Could a massive eruption cause an ice age? Has this happened in the past? Can we find answers to questions like this? Where would we go to look for evidence?

—Adapted from NASA Facts #220, March 1994

The Story—Part 4

DISCOVERY FILE

Out-of-This-World Volcanoes

Here on Earth there are hundreds of active volcanoes—a clue that our planet is still alive, geologically speaking. But Earth is not alone. Evidence of volcanic activity has been sighted on several other planets spread across the solar system. Studying volcanoes on these distant globes can help us learn more about how volcanoes work on Earth. This is a discipline called *comparative planetology*.

Thanks to telescopes and space probes, we now know that volcanoes play a crucial part in the evolution of many planets and their moons.

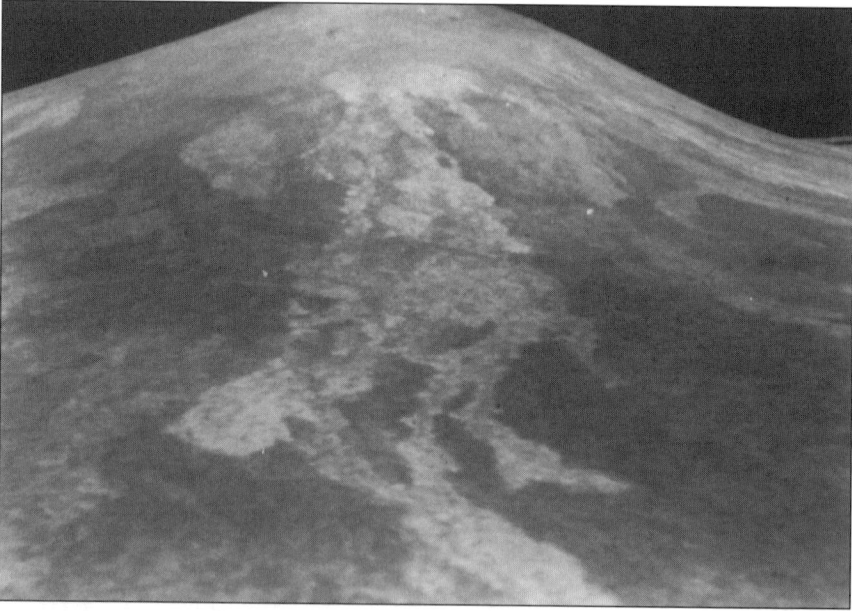

The surface of Venus.

Lunar Volcanoes

The rocky surface of Earth's Moon shows that it underwent a period of volcanism from 3 to 4 billion years ago. As one example, dark areas on the Moon, called *seas* or *maria*, are the products of ancient basalt-lava flows. Other lunar features point to volcanoes at work in the Moon's ancient past. Today, there are no active volcanoes on the Moon.

On Mercury

Having features similar to the Moon's, tiny Mercury also looks as if volcanic lava flows helped shaped its surface.

Venus—Hot, Hot, Hot

The inhospitable surface of the planet Venus is dotted with volcanoes. Scientists can't see Venus' surface because it is covered by a thick layer of clouds. However, the Venusian atmosphere was pierced by radar signals from the U.S. *Magellan* spacecraft. One of the largest shield volcanoes in the solar system was detected by *Magellan's* radar as it mapped 98 percent of Venus' surface between 1990 and 1994. Automated landers built by Russia have touched down on Venus. Pictures relayed from the surface showed a relatively smooth landscape, perhaps formed by lava flows or pyroclas-

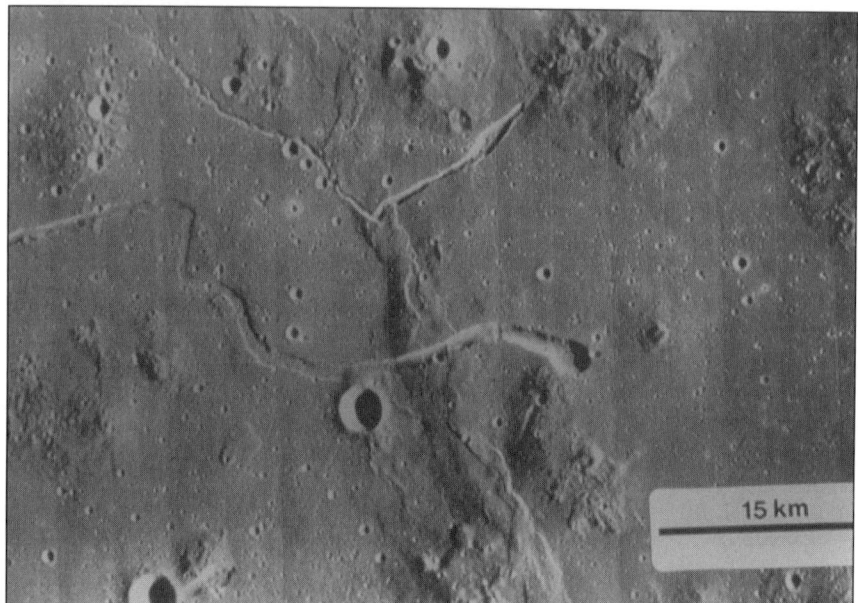

The surface of Mercury.

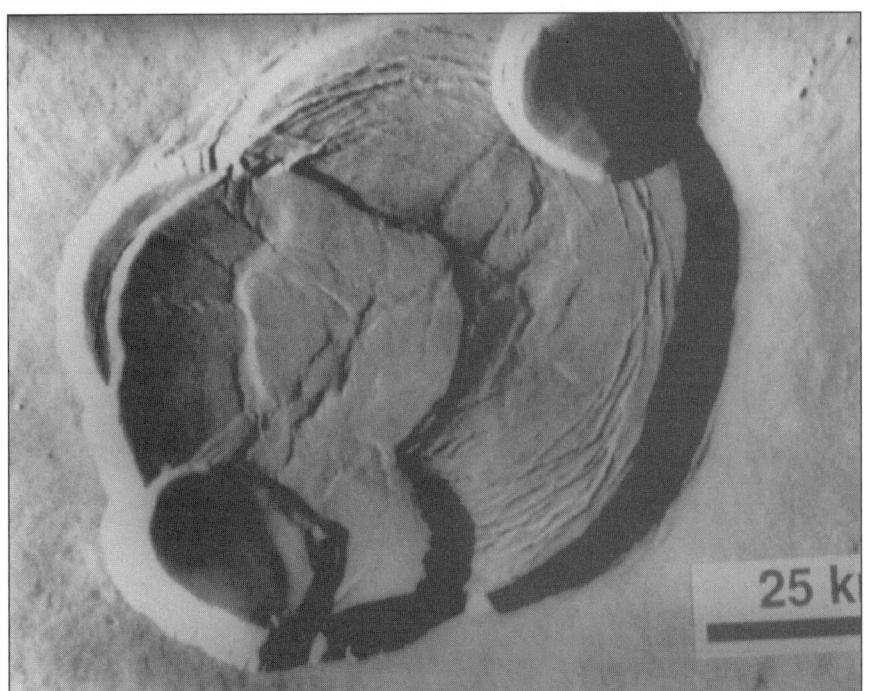

A volcano on Mars.

Icy Volcanoes on Neptune's Triton

The ice geysers on Neptune's moon, Triton, are considered the volcanic oddball of the solar system. A *Voyager* spacecraft captured images of these strange erupting features on Triton.

As future spacecraft explore other niches within the solar system, still more volcanic features may be discovered. Could there be volcanoes on planets orbiting other stars in the galaxy? Most likely the answer will be yes.

tic deposits. Volcanoes on Venus may be spewing out lava as you read this.

Mars' Mighty Volcanoes

The largest volcano detected in the solar system is located on Mars. The mighty Olympus Mons is shaped like a huge shield volcano. It dwarfs Mount Everest, the highest peak on Earth, and Mauna Loa, the largest volcano on our home planet. A number of Martian volcanoes have been imaged by spacecraft, although none of them appears active.

Jupiter's Io—The "Pizza" Moon

Jupiter's moon Io is dotted with active volcanic plumes. This fact was documented by the U.S. *Voyagers* 1 and 2 spacecraft when they flew by the Jovian moon. Io is currently the most volcanically active body known. The erupting moon takes on the appearance of a colossal pizza with splotches of black against surface colors of yellow, orange, black, and white.

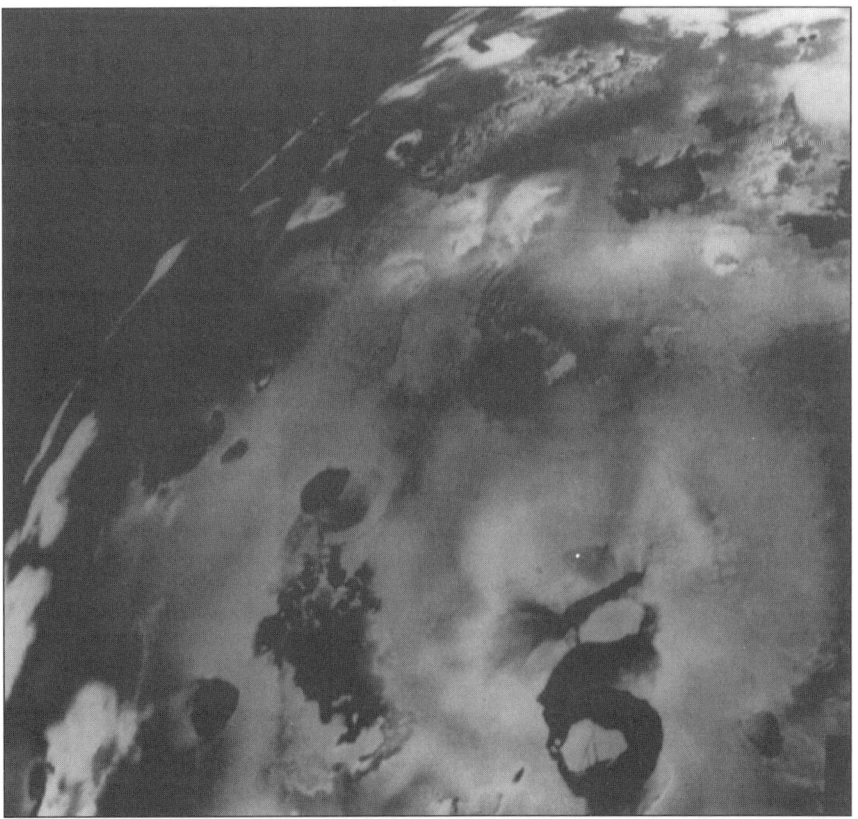

Volcanic plumes on Io.

The Story—Part 4

Discovery File

Hot Tips for Living with Volcanoes

If you live near a volcano, what can you do to prepare for an eruption? Plan ahead. Planning ahead can protect you from an eruption that could start at any time, day or night. Don't forget, volcanoes interrupt water supplies, clog sewers, block roads, and cut off electrical power and telephone service.

Here are a few tips to prepare yourself.

- Know your area. Is there a threat of volcanic activity? If you live or work where there is a likelihood of a volcanic eruption, think about the actions you or your family might take.
- Know the plans your local officials have for warning and evacuating your area if that becomes necessary.
- If an eruption begins, wait for public officials to contact you. Don't call them. Too many incoming calls can prevent officials from helping the largest number of people.
- You may be told to stay indoors, so keep extra water and food around in case your area becomes temporarily cut off. If you are told to leave, make sure there's plenty of fuel in your car. The electricity to your home may be cut off, so have a battery-operated radio handy for receiving emergency messages.
- When an eruption is in progress, sudden explosions are possible, and it is quite hazardous! Stay away from the volcano! This is not the time for sightseeing. Wait until scientists and local officials designate safe viewing sites. Don't ignore roadblocks and enter closed areas. Doing so might put your life in danger.
- In the event that ash is spewing from a volcano, avoid downwind areas. A building can offer protection from falling ash. But a building may not protect you from a pyroclastic flow or ash hurricane. Flying rocks may break windows and even set fire to a building. The only guarantee of safety is to heed warnings and leave dangerous areas before eruptions begin.
- Volcanic debris flows can occur even when there is no volcanic activity. The danger from a debris flow increases near streams and decreases as you move toward higher ground. Debris flows can move faster than you can run.

Eruption blasts material into the atmosphere.

By Austin Post, USGS

DISCOVERY FILE

Myths and Beliefs about Volcanoes

Where did the word *volcano* come from? The word was first used by people who lived near the small island of Vulcano in the Mediterranean Sea near Italy and Sicily. Centuries ago, these people believed Vulcano was the chimney of the forge of Vulcan, the Roman god of fire and metalworking. (Besides *volcano*, the word *vulcan* survives today in the word *vulcanize*. Do you see a connection?)

As the mountain rumbled and erupted, spewing out hot lava and clouds of dust, the people thought Vulcan was beating out thunderbolts for Jupiter, king of the gods, and weapons for Mars, the god of war.

In Polynesia, people attributed erupting volcanoes to the beautiful but wrathful Pele, their goddess of volcanoes. A gushing volcano, Polynesians believed, clearly meant Pele was very angry.

Hawaiians also have another myth about the goddess Pele: she stomps on the ground to make earthquakes when aggravated. Her rage also evokes boiling surges of lava from deep underground. Pele rides the molten and destructive wave of lava, screaming curses and tossing fiery boulders while swallowing everything in her way.

Some Hawaiian islanders remain fearful of Pele. They respect her fiery nature but believe she can be appeased if they cast offerings of sacred ohelo berries and other items into the lava. Even scientists show respect to Pele. They use the term *Pele's hair* to describe a formation of very thin threads of lava that have been whipped by the wind, looking very much like strands of hair.

Today, of course, we know volcanic eruptions involve more fact than myth and can be studied and interpreted by scientists and students.

IN THE NEWS

Volcano evacuees home today

By Juan J. Walte
USA TODAY

The first group of relatives of U.S. airmen and sailors stationed in the Philippines arrives on the West Coast today, fleeing from a gigantic volcanic eruption that damaged the two largest U.S. bases in Asia.

At least 101 people have been killed, including the child of a U.S. enlisted man. The Philippine government estimated 180,000 people were chased from their homes.

The evacuees landing at McChord Air Force Base in Tacoma, Wash., are among 20,000 military family members leaving the Philippines in a huge pullout involving 17 warships as well as cargo planes.

"It's been horrible this past week," said Lisa Hedland of Ware, Mass., wife of Air Force Sgt. Jeff Hedland from Clark Air Base, as she prepared to board the cruiser Long Beach at Subic Bay Naval Station with her 15-month-old daughter.

Clark and Subic Bay are the oldest and largest U.S. military facilities on foreign soil, and their future — now more uncertain than ever — is the subject of long negotiations between Washington and Manila.

The U.S. Pacific Command said the Navy ships, including two aircraft carrier groups, are taking evacuees from Subic Bay to the southern city of Cebu. From there, C-141 transport planes have begun to fly the families to McChord.

The two carriers — Abraham Lincoln, the Navy's newest carrier, and Midway, the Navy's oldest — are either at or en route to Subic Bay to help with the evacuation.

There has been no estimate of overall damage to the bases, but the figure could easily run into the millions of dollars:

▶ Clark, located 8½ miles east of the volcano, is covered by 10 to 12 inches of ash, and numerous buildings have been damaged. Roads there are clogged with ash and mud.

▶ At Subic Bay, 50 miles south of the volcano, tons of ash cover roofs, roads and harbor facilities. Water and power have been disrupted.

Scientists, meanwhile, said the worst of Mount Pinatubo's eruptions appear to be over.

But more trouble may be ahead: Experts say the volcano Taal, 40 miles south of Manila, is displaying abnormal activity.

HOT LINE NUMBERS
Toll-free telephone numbers for information about U.S. armed services members in the Philippines:
▶ **Air Force:** 1-800-253-9276 (8 a.m.-midnight EDT)
▶ **Navy:** 1-800-255-3808 (24 hours)
▶ **Marine Corps:** 1-800-874-7454 (7:30 a.m.-5 p.m. EDT)

By Dave Schad, AP
DEPARTING SUBIC BAY: U.S. military dependents board the refrigerator ship Spica on Monday. They will be taken to the southern Philippine island of Cebu, then flown to Tacoma, Wash.

IN THE NEWS

U.S. media ignore human suffering caused by volcanic eruptions

I gazed up at thousands of bewildered evacuees' faces in Manila's Amoranto Stadium and felt absolutely helpless.

Under the sweltering sun, families vied for space to sit or lie on concrete seats, many still dazed from the rigors of their flight from Mount Pinatubo's wrath.

As I listened to the evacuation center coordinator's briefing, I realized for the first time the human scale of destruction that these violent eruptions had wreaked upon the lives of the men, women and children in this stadium and other evacuation centers.

Deprived of homes and sources of living, Pinatubo's victims face a numbing future.

There is no potable water. Ashes, sand and mud disgorged from the volcano have polluted rivers, wells and water reservoirs as far away as Manila.

There is no electricity in many areas around the volcano, so factories and businesses have been brought to a standstill.

There are few trees left standing and few homes with intact roofs because ash and sand, mixed with the monsoon season's constant rain, create a concrete-like substance that causes whole structures to collapse.

Irene Natividad is executive director of the Philippine American Foundation and former chair of the National Women's Political Caucus.

IRENE NATIVIDAD

There are few farms left, buried as they are under highly acidic ash deposits or, worse, sand from the volcano.

The highly productive prawn and fish farms are also gone, while mango and coconut groves are predicted to take two to four years before they can bear fruit again.

There is nothing benign or scenic about a volcanic eruption: 338 people have died and 200,000 have fled their homes. For many, a way of life is gone. The daily terror of ongoing eruptions with their accompanying "rain" of ash and sand, earthquake tremors (now numbering well over 100), the noxious fumes of sulfuric gases and the constant threat of mud flows, which can erase a whole town, make planning a new life difficult.

The fear I felt as my hotel room rocked several times when Mount Pinatubo first erupted violently and blanketed Manila with ash is nowhere near the terror that plagued the evacuees closer to the volcano itself. The isolation and frustration I felt as closed airports in Manila and Hong Kong left me stranded are nowhere near the permanent personal and economic dislocation of Mount Pinatubo's victims.

Now, safe at home in the United States for a scant week, I am amazed by the lack of mention here of the human toll of this disaster. There has been wide coverage of the volcano's impact on U.S. bases, the evacuation of U.S. dependents and scientific assessments of the eruptions by experts. *The New York Times'* front-page piece June 30 on the volcano's positive effect on retarding global warming left me enraged. While I'm happy California will now get the rain it needs because of Pinatubo's ash clouds, I am appalled by the lack of reports on the plight of the Filipino farmer who must now confront a highly acidic soil on which rice — the staple of the Philippine diet — may never grow. Where is the Filipino face in this disaster?

The fact of the matter is that the largest volcanic eruption in the 20th century has caused massive economic and environmental damage to a people just beginning to recover from two prior natural disasters — last year's earthquake and massive typhoon.

How to deal with the potential of acid rain, the effect of sulfur-laden ashes on people and animals and the deforestation of large tracts of land are just some of the environmental concerns now confronting Filipinos.

I am told that nature is resilient. And so are Filipinos. Already, plans are under way for massive cleanup efforts, for new relocation areas charted for the evacuees and for research into new crops and sources of livelihood — all this while ashfall, mud flows and tremors continue.

Volcanologists say that Mount Pinatubo could be in a continuous state of eruption for as long as three years. In the meantime, Americans — a people compassionate by nature — need to be aware of and respond to the ongoing human suffering inflicted by this volcano. Otherwise, how can we look the Filipino children in Amoranto Stadium in the face when they ask: "When do we go home?"

INTERDISCIPLINARY ACTIVITY

Math: Volcanoes and Volume

Purpose
To determine the ratio between the radius and height of a volcano, and also to calculate the amount of material *(ejecta)* that could be released during an eruption.

Background
A television program about volcanoes is being developed by the Washington State Department of Safety. As state mathematician, you have been asked to calculate the amount of material *(ejecta)* that can be released from a volcano. Because Mount St. Helens was recently active, you will use that example.

During the spectacular May 18, 1980 eruption of Mount St. Helens, molten material exploded from the volcano. Much of this material rose as high as 14 miles (20 km) into the air. It was blown eastward by high winds, and eventually fell as volcanic ash on fields, towns, and cities to the east of the volcano.

In addition to molten material shooting out of the volcano's summit, a massive landslide, called a *debris flow*, swept down the north side of the mountain and left a large hole! The debris flow, composed of rock, mud, and ice, swept into local streams. It filled riverbeds, damaged bridges, and killed plants and wildlife.

Before the eruption, Mount St. Helens looked more or less cone-shaped. After the eruption it still had a cone-shaped base, but it also had an enormous crater on its northern side. What was the volume of the material lost?

The show needs only a rough estimate, so you have decided to simplify the problem. Volcanoes are basically cone-shaped, so you will first estimate the volume of the entire volcano. Then you will estimate the amount of ejecta (in cubic feet) released.

To calculate the volume of a cone, you need the radius and the height, but the only measurement you have for Mount St. Helens is its height. Therefore, in this activity you will do an experiment that will help you calculate the approximate radius of the base of Mount St. Helens. You will use the mathematical concepts of ratios, proportions, and the volume of a cone to help you determine the volume of the entire mountain.

Finally, you will estimate the fraction of the total volume that was lost when the north side of Mount St. Helens collapsed.

Materials
For each student or group:
- Bucket of sand
- Box
- Metric ruler

Procedure
First, you must determine the approximate ratio between the radius of the base (assume it is circular) and the height of a volcano. To determine this ratio, you will make several models of different sizes.

For each model, pour a pile of sand in a box. Measure the height and radius of the conical pile. Repeat this procedure four or five times, and then find the average value of the radius/height relationship.

Assuming Mount St. Helens is basically conical in shape with a height of 8,300 feet, use the concept of proportion to estimate its radius. Hint: radius of sand/height of sand=radius of Mount St. Helens/height of Mount St. Helens.

$$\frac{r_{sand}}{h_{sand}} = \frac{r_{Mt.\ SH}}{h_{Mt.\ SH}}$$

Next, determine the volume of Mount St. Helens. The volume of a cone equals one-third pi (π) times the product of the radius of the base squared and its height ($V = \frac{1}{3}\pi\ r^2 h$).

Finally, assuming that 5 percent of the total volume of Mount St. Helens was released as ejecta, determine the total number of cubic feet of ejecta that was released.

Conclusion
Prepare a graphic that the producers of the television show can use. Your graphic can be in the form of a poster on which you draw a picture of Mount St. Helens and show the number of cubic feet of ejecta released.

Just in case the television producer decides to interview you on camera, be prepared to discuss some of the errors that may be involved in your calculations.

INTERDISCIPLINARY ACTIVITY

Social Studies: Hot Spots

Purpose
To gather information on volcanoes and to create a map showing the world's major volcanoes.

Background
An eccentric multimillionaire wants to invest a large sum of money in a new theme park. The theme of the park will be a volcano, and a real volcano will be the main attraction. Interested developers must submit a well-documented plan for the park. Since the park will attract visitors from all nations, the park may be located anywhere in the world. The only requirement is that the site must contain a real volcano.

Materials
- Research materials (library)
- World atlas (one for the class)
- Construction paper, other art materials

Procedure
Research a specific volcano using resources that are available in the library and write a brief report explaining why the site you have chosen is the best in the world for the theme park. (The teacher might provide you with a specific volcanic site.)

Along with the written presentation, create an advertising brochure that promotes the park as an attractive amusement/vacation paradise. Include in the brochure the following information: continent, country, latitude, longitude, and type of volcano. You and the other park developers will present your findings and brochures to the class orally. The volcanic site will be located and marked (with a red dot) on a large map of the world displayed for all to see.

When all presentations have been given, you will examine the locations of volcanoes on the world map. Do you see a pattern? Compare the class map showing the locations of volcanoes to a map showing the locations of plate boundaries. What is the relationship between these features?

INTERDISCIPLINARY ACTIVITY

Technology Education: Air Cruisin'!

Purpose
To design and build an air-cushioned vehicle (ACV), better known as a Hovercraft™.

Background
Officials from Washington State have hired a media-production company to produce after-school television specials about Mount Rainier and other volcanoes in the state. The production company has surveyed the locations to be filmed and discovered that a conventional vehicle cannot be used there because of the volcanic ash, rocks, mud, and snow. This is where you come in. Your company, Wild Things, Inc., is known for specialized vehicle design and manufacturing. The film company needs a vehicle that will safely carry their equipment over the rugged Mount Rainier terrain. After intensive research, you have decided an ACV is the best choice.

Your assignment: design and construct an ACV/Hovercraft™ to the specifications permitted.

Materials
For each student or group:
- Sketch paper
- Graph paper
- Pencil
- Scissors and/or mat knife
- Mat board or some form of cardboard (not too thick)
- Sewing thread spool (not too large)
- Strong adhesive (example: Liquid Nails™)
- Balloon (preferably round)
- Compass
- Protractor

Procedure
1. Research ACVs/Hovercrafts™—their shapes, designs, and so on.
2. Sketch some possible top views of an ACV. Select one design (maximum size is 8 ½ inches × 11 inches).
3. Fold your graph paper in half lengthwise and draw one half of your top view against the fold of the graph paper.
4. If you are satisfied with your design, cut it out while it is folded (you now have a symmetrical design).
5. Transfer the graph-paper design to the mat board or cardboard and cut this out with scissors or a mat knife. (Note: If you are using a mat knife, put some additional cardboard underneath so you do not cut into the tabletop).
6. Locate center lines in both directions and draw them on your design.
7. Mark and drill a hole in the center of the design that is the same size as the center hole in your thread spool. Use the drill press or whatever your teacher permits.
8. Use an adhesive approved by the teacher. Apply some on the bottom of the spool and attach it over the hole in your ACV. Allow it to dry overnight. When the adhesive is dry, paint or decorate your ACV.
9. Blow up a round balloon and pinch it closed while you wrap the end around the top of the spool.
10. Release the balloon. What happens? Do you need to make any modifications?

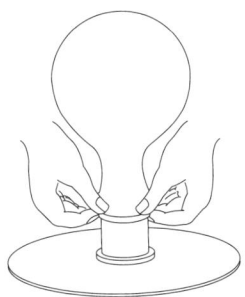

Conclusion
1. What do you know about ACVs/Hovercrafts™?
2. Why did or didn't your design work?
3. How well did other designs of your classmates float?
4. Did some shapes work better than others? Why or why not?
5. What would you do differently if given another chance?
6. How do technology, science, and math affect this activity and ACV design?
7. How do you think this would work with a motor, propeller, and rudder? What might happen if you tried?
8. Would a shroud or skirt around your ACV help? Why or why not?
9. Would a different size or shape of balloon make a difference? Why or why not?
10. Would a different hole placement make a difference?

Interdisciplinary Activity

Writing: Volcano!

Technical or report writing is not the only purpose of writing. Many writers use the written word to express their own emotions or their own creativity. After your activities related to the scientific study of volcanoes, do one or more of the following expressive writing activities:

1. Now that you have studied historical impacts of volcanoes and researched the processes and hazards related to volcanoes, think about the reactions you had as you considered these events and possible future events. What feelings did you have as you read about past eruptions or considered future eruptions? How might these volcanoes relate to other events you have experienced in your own life? Write a paragraph in which you explain your previous experiences with, personal reactions to, and new understandings of the effects of volcanoes.

2. Suppose you were one of the few survivors of a historical volcanic eruption. Write a letter to a friend in another country in which you describe your personal reactions to the devastation and disaster.

3. You are thrilled that you are one of the few Earthlings who can communicate with the extraterrestrial Zortarians. After decoding their message (see Science Activity "Do You Tire of Fire?" on pages 49-50), you and your team have provided them with the scientific data they requested. But now you want to tell them more about your life on Earth and ask them questions about their lives. Using the Zortarian alphabet, write a letter asking your Zortarian colleagues about themselves.

4. Because of the emotional impact of the awesome power of natural events, many poets describe events such as storms, earthquakes, and volcanoes. Write a poem in which you express the potential power of an inactive volcano.

Performance Assessment

Writing to Persuade

Directions
Complete the writing activity below. Read the prompt carefully. You may refer to all your previous work in this unit.

Prompt
As the public information officer of your media production company, you have decided that in addition to your after-school television special, the state of Washington should be doing more to alert all citizens to the power of volcanoes. You want to persuade state officials to extend your media company's campaign to promote public awareness of potential hazards.

Write a letter in which you persuade state officials that a broader media campaign is needed. Before you write, recall the reasons for your believing that this additional campaign is needed. Be prepared to include in your letter the reasons for your concern and the facts that support your reasons.

Remember to include the evidence your production company has gathered on the effects, hazards, benefits, monitoring, and predictability of volcanoes. Consider ways in which your firm could inform citizens about volcanic activity without unnecessarily alarming them.

Organize your information so it will be logical and persuasive. Your letter should show that you have a clear understanding of the issues and should use clear, correct, and convincing language. The letter should persuade state officials to authorize your firm to mount a new statewide information campaign on volcanoes.

As you write you may want to do the following:
- Use a graphic organizer or prewriting strategy, such as listing or webbing, to organize supporting data, evidence, and logical arguments. Then use these ideas to write a rough draft.
- Evaluate your letter using the Peer-Response Form on page 62. Keep in mind that you are writing a business letter. Then get your peers to evaluate and react, using the same form.
- Revise your work, taking into consideration the responses given during the evaluation of your writing.
- Look over your work. Proofread your letter using the Proofreading Guidesheet on page 63 and prepare a final copy of your work.

Peer-Response Form

Directions

1. Ask your partners to listen carefully as you read your rough draft aloud.

2. Ask your partners to help you improve your writing by telling you their answers to the questions below.

3. Jot down notes about what your partners say:

    a. What did you like best about my rough draft?

    b. What did you have the hardest time understanding in my rough draft?

    c. What can you suggest that I do to improve my rough draft?

4. Exchange rough drafts with a partner. In pencil, place a check mark near any mechanical, spelling, or grammatical constructions about which you are uncertain. Return the papers and check your own. Ask your partner for clarification if you do not understand or agree with the comments on your paper. Jot down notes you want to remember when writing your revision.

Proofreading Guidesheet

1. Have you identified the assigned purpose of the writing assignment and have you accomplished this purpose?

2. Have you written on the assigned topic?

3. Have you identified the assigned form your writing should take and have you written accordingly?

4. Have you addressed the assigned audience in your writing?

5. Have you used sentences of different lengths and types to make your writing effective?

6. Have you chosen language carefully so the reader understands what you mean?

7. Have you made your writing clear for someone else to read by:

   - using appropriate capitalization?
   - keping pronouns clear?
   - keeping verb tense consistent?
   - making sure all words are spelled correctly?
   - using correct punctuation?
   - using complete sentences?
   - making all subjects and verbs agree?
   - organizing your ideas into logical paragraphs?

RESOURCES

Books

Aylesworth, Thomas G., and Virginia L. Aylesworth. *The Mount St. Helens Disaster: What We've Learned*. New York: Franklin Watts, 1983. (Advanced level)

Barrett, Norman. *Volcanoes* (Picture Library series). New York: Franklin Watts, 1990.

Decker, Robert W., and Barbara B. Decker. *Mountains of Fire: The Nature of Volcanoes*. New York: Cambridge University Press, 1991.

The Diagram Group and David Lambert. *The Field Guide to Geology*. New York: Facts on File, 1989.

Erickson, Jon. *Volcanoes and Earthquakes*. Blue Ridge Summit, Penn.: TAB Books, Inc., 1987.

Krafft, Maurice. *Volcanoes: Fire from the Earth* (The Discovery Series). New York: Harry M. Abrams, Inc., 1993.

[The Kraffts died while photographing the eruption of Unzen in Japan on June 3, 1991. They are featured in the video *Valley of 10,000 Smokes* in the *National Geographic Explorer* series that aired on June 26, 1994, on TBS.]

Lane, Frank W. *The Violent Earth*. Topsfield, Mass.: Salem House, 1986.

Lauber, Patricia. Volcano: *The Eruption and Healing of Mount St. Helens*. New York: Aladdin Books, Macmillan Children's Group, 1993.

Grove, Noel. "Volcanoes: Crucibles of Creation." *National Geographic*, Vol. 182, No. 6 (December 1992), pp. 5–41, 144, 154).

"Volcanoes: Scorching Hot to Icy Cold!" *Odyssey Magazine*, Vol. 2, No. 1., Jan/Feb, 1993.

O'Meara, Stephen, and Donna O'Meara. *Volcanoes: Passion and Fury*. Cambridge, Mass.: Sky Publishing, 1994.

Planet Earth Volcano. Alexandria, Va.: Time-Life Books, Inc., 1982.

Taylor, Barbara. *Mountains and Volcanoes* (Young Discoverers Series). Las Vegas: Kingfisher Books, 1993.

Taylor, Jeffrey. *Volcanoes in Our Solar System*. New York: Dodd, Mead, 1983.

Van Cleave, Janice. Janice Van Cleave's *Volcanoes: Mind-Boggling Experiments You Can Turn into Science Fair Projects* (Spectacular Science Projects series). New York: John Wiley & Sons, Inc., 1994. (ages 8–12)

Van Rose, Susanna, and Ian F. Mercer. *Volcanoes*. London: British Museum (Natural History), 1991.

Vogt, Gregory. *Volcanoes*. New York: Franklin Watts, 1993.

Watt, Fiona. *Earthquakes and Volcanoes* (Understanding Geography series). Tulsa, Okla.: Educational Development Corp., 1994.

Wenkam, Robert. *The Edge of Fire: Volcano and Earthquake Country in Western North America and Hawaii*. San Francisco: Sierra Club Books, 1987.

Woods, Jenny. *Volcanoes*. New York: Puffin Books, Penguin, 1990. (ages 8–12)

Videos

Mount Pinatubo: In the Path of the Killer Volcano.

> The science of predicting volcanoes in the Philippines during the 1992 eruption of Mount Pinatubo.
>
> One hour, *NOVA* series from PBS.

Nature: The Volcano Watchers.

> About the famous French volcanologists Maurice and Katia Krafft.
>
> One hour, #PBS-103, from PBS.

Fire on the Rim.

> Four-part video series on volcanoes, earthquakes, and the cultures of the Pacific Rim.

Episode Three: The Prediction Problem.

One hour, PBS.

VolcanoScapes I: Pelée's March to the Pacific!

VolcanoScapes II: Hawaii's Kilauea Volcano Rages On!

Tropical Visions Video, Inc., 62 Halaulani Place, Hilo, HI 96720

Internet
Volcano World
http://volcano.und.nodak.edu/

Modern and near real time volcano information, draws extensively on remote sensing images (AVHRR, Landsat TM, Magellan, Gloria), and other data collections. Ask a Volcanologist; How to become a Volcanologist; Current and Recent Eruptions; Images of Volcanoes Hawaiian Tour Guide; Mount St. Helens; Volcano Lessons; Volcano Slide Show

Information about volcanoes is also available from

U.S. Department of the Interior/U.S. Geological Survey

U.S. Government Printing Office, Superintendent of Documents, Mail Stop: SSOP, Washington, DC 20402-9328.

Titles include: "Volcanic and Seismic Hazards on the Island of Hawaii" (#1992-0-333-230 QL2), "Monitoring Active Volcanoes" (#1993-348-979), and "Volcanic Hazards at Mount Shasta, California" (#1993-350-086).

Acknowledgments

Author
Russell G. Wright, with contributions from Janet West Crampton, Leonard David, Barbara Sprungman, and the following teachers:

Science Activities
Eugene M. Molesky, Ridgeview Middle School, Gaithersburg, MD
Frank S. Weisel, Poolesville Junior/Senior High School, Poolesville, MD

Teacher Advisors
Nancy A. Carey, Col. E. Brooke Lee Middle School, Silver Spring, MD
Charles E. Doebler, Robert Frost Middle School, Rockville, MD
Nell Jeter, Earle B. Wood Middle School, Rockville, MD
Richard Knight, Baker Middle School, Damascus, MD
William R. Krayer, Gaithersburg High School, Gaithersburg, MD
Robert McDowell, Albert Einstein High School, Kensington, MD
Sheila Shillinger, Montgomery Village Middle School, Gaithersburg, MD
Thomas G. Smith, Briggs Chaney Middle School, Silver Spring, MD

Interdisciplinary Activities
Bernard J. Hudock, Watkins Mill High School, Gaithersburg, MD
Jeanne S. Klugel, Col. E. Brooke Lee Middle School, Silver Spring, MD
Joseph M. Panarella, Montgomery Village Middle School, Gaithersburg, MD
John Senuta, Ridgeview Middle School, Gaithersburg, MD

Teacher-Writer Interns
Kelly Hortch and Donna Obermeier, University of Maryland, College Park, MD

Geology Advisor
Evan D. Wolff, Northern Arizona University, Flagstaff, AZ

Volcanology Advisor
James Luhr, Smithsonian Institution, Washington, DC

Event/Site Support
Captain Mike Ryan, Air Force Military Personnel Center, Randolph Air Force Base, TX

Student Consultants
Ridgeview Intermediate School, Gaithersburg, MD
  James Cherubim, Dustin Doyle, Valthea Fry, Amy Gold, Mishell Hashmi, Eric Hickerson, Farid Jahanmir, Eric Linden, Ligia Lorenzana, Brian Martin, Neha Mehta, Jennifer Norris, Cory Nye
Tilden Middle School, Rockville, MD
  William Wright
New Market Middle School, Frederick County, MD
  Lauren Molesky

Field-Test Teachers
Judith Basile and Karen Shugrue, Agawam Junior High School, Feeding Hills, MA
David Needham and Gloria Yost, Albert Einstein Middle School, Sacramento, CA
Adrianne Criminger, Lanier Middle School, Buford, GA
Cheryl Glotfelty and Linda Mosser, Northern Middle School, Accident, MD
Kevin Feeney, Northeast Middle School, Baltimore, MD
Mark Carlson and Amy Resler, Westlane Middle School, Indianapolis, IN

EBS Advisory Committee
Dr. Eddie Anderson, National Aeronautic and Space Administration
Ms. Mary Ann Brearton, American Association for the Advancement of Science
Dr. Lynn Dierking, Science Learning, Inc.
Mr. Bob Dubill, *USA Today*
Mr. Herbert Freiberger, United States Geological Survey
Ms. Joyce Gross, National Oceanic and Atmospheric Administration
Dr. Harry Herzer, National Aeronautic and Space Administration
Dr. Frank Ireton, American Geophysical Union
Mr. Bill Krayer, Gaithersburg High School
Dr. Rocky Lopes, American Red Cross
Dr. Jerry Lynch, John T. Baker Middle School
Ms. Marilyn P. MacCabe, Federal Emergency Management Agency
Ms. Virginia Major, United States Geological Survey
Mr. John Ortman, United States Department of Energy
Dr. Noel Raufasté, Jr., National Institute of Standards and Technology
Dr. Bill Sacco, Trianalytics Corporation
Mr. Ron Slotkin, United States Environmental Protection Agency
Ms. Katarina Stenstedt, Addison-Wesley Publishing Co.
Ms. Linda Straka, Federal Emergency Management Agency